Love, Styled

Sometimes your heart needs a makeover.

Michelle Tibbs-Brown

For my parents who taught me the importance of the written word.

To all my favorite people... thank you for the encouragement.

Chapter 1

Margaux burst through the door, causing Elle to jump.

"It happened! I can't believe it happened." Margaux had excitement pulsing through her small frame as she was jumping up and down in front of Elle, her new boss.

Elle was thinking how thankful she was that she had just finished with her last client, and that they were the only two people in the small shop. "What happened?" Elle asked calmly, hoping that her tone would take Margaux down a bit in her excitement. Elle was shocked to realize she was sounding like someone's grandma, even if only in her thoughts. "Soooo, what happened? I thought you just went to get a latte?" Elle asked again, this time taking a step toward Margaux and offering a calming hand on her shoulder while Margaux attempted to catch her breath.

"Well, I heard about a contest on radio WQHT that could give a listener VIP tickets to the *Echo Chamber* movie tonight … annnnnnd … I won them! I can't believe I won. I just have to leave, pick up the tickets from the radio station, run by the thrift store for something to wear that isn't covered in hair clippings, and go to the premiere! Squeeeee … I can't believe it!" Margaux was jumping up and down now and hugging her new boss.

Sadly, Elle didn't know when the appropriate time was to remind Margaux that she was set to close the shop tonight for the first time since getting hired. Elle reminded herself that Margaux was new to New York and was excited about *everything*. Elle reminded herself that Margaux's enthusiasm was one of her best qualities and one of the reasons she hired her a few weeks ago as her new stylist. Elle then considered that all she had planned tonight was to spend time with her cat and catch up on a Netflix series. Eventually, Elle promised herself that she would get a life that didn't revolve around work, a life once she had a thriving business in her new neighborhood; meanwhile, work would be her life for a bit longer. Elle's thoughts were consumed by her own obligations, and her face couldn't help but show it.

Suddenly, Margaux's face fell, remembering her responsibilities at the hair salon that night. She remembered the hours of training that Elle spent showing Margaux how to close the business, and it was her first night to be trusted to do so. Elle had prepared Margaux for this and in her excitement, she completely forgot about it … until now. Margaux brushed one of her blonde curls behind her ear, as she was prone to do when she was thinking.

Elle noticed Margaux's excitement fade and asked her, "What happened? Where's the excitement?"

"I just remembered; I am supposed to close the shop tonight. You have spent hours preparing me for this, and I completely spaced it with excitement. I didn't think I would *win* the tickets, but I had to try. I am sorry that I completely forgot about it in my enthusiasm. Do you want to go for me if the radio station will allow it?" Margaux stood in front of Elle with a hopeful expression on her face.

Elle's decision to send Margaux to the premiere was made five minutes before when she saw the joy in Margaux's face after sharing her exciting news. "No, Margaux, I will close tonight. I have some paperwork to do and don't have anyone else scheduled in the shop this evening. It will give me a chance to work on some budget details. Don't worry, you can close another time."

Margaux practically tackled Elle with a hug. She started jumping up and down enthusiastically, with her blonde curly hair bouncing as she jumped. Most of the time, Elle felt like her new employee's sister; well, she was her *only* employee. However, seeing Margaux's thrill, she felt like she had maturity beyond her years. Elle longed to have that excitement again like Margaux and reassured Margaux, "You go and have a great time. I promise that you will close again soon. Go have fun, and be sure to take pictures for me, ok? Besides, all the celebrity stuff you love so much is a waste of time to me. These famous people should really use their influence to help others." Margaux mouthed silently "help others" at the same time as Elle; she had heard the spiel before tonight.

Elle liked to remind her that her gossip magazines were a bit ridiculous, but Margaux didn't care. She moved to NYC to see and experience exactly what she was doing tonight. Margaux had the ideal small-town upbringing but longed for more when she moved to New York. Thankfully, Margaux can't believe how fortunate she was to find a boss like Elle. "Thank you, thank you, thank you," she cooed as she grabbed her things for a quick exit.

Elle walked her to the door to say goodbye as though she was a visitor at her house. "Be safe. Don't accept a drink from a stranger. Text me if you go anywhere unusual. Have fun. I can't wait to hear about it tomorrow." Elle noticed rain coming down lightly as she helped Margaux out the shop door. "Be safe with this rain too because it is harder to see pedestrians at night," Elle shouted as Margaux was already ten feet down the sidewalk.

"Got it. Thanks, and I'll send some pictures," Margaux called over her shoulder as she quickly made her way down the sidewalk, smiling from ear to ear as she was about to experience her first NYC VIP event.

Elle turned around and looked at the small space, the little shop she loved. Elle dreamed of owning a shop like this and she felt a small sense of pride wash over her as she took in her tiny space that she lovingly created. They had only been open for three months in this up-and-coming neighborhood, but it had promise. Elle had been avoiding her budget because she knew that the kind offer, she was given for a discounted rent for three months was soon ending. She needed to make sure she could pay rent and pay Margaux. Elle had some savings and could avoid paying herself if she needed to do so for a bit longer but rent and Margaux were at the top of the list when it came to paying the bills. Elle's dad's disapproving comments began to invade her mind as she looked over some of her expenses while sitting down at the desk in the back room. The reality of how tight her budget weighed heavily on her. Although Elle was actually good at budgeting, some of these unexpected costs like hiring a professional painter and plumber were a surprise as she opened this shop and made her new endeavor even more costly. As she returned to reviewing the expense reports, Elle thought she heard something and paused for a moment. Reassured that she didn't hear anything, she then heard a slight knock at the door.

This was a new-to-her neighborhood, and she wasn't complete-ly confident that it was always safe. After being robbed at her last location, Elle had become extra cautious when alone at the shop. She was sure that she locked the door when Margaux left and ap-proached the door cautiously when she heard another knock, louder and faster. Elle remembered that she kept extra umbrellas there and figured Margaux most likely returned to borrow one. Elle grabbed an umbrella just as she was approaching the door. "You must need this," and pushed an umbrella into the face of the person standing before her, thinking she was going to see Margaux.

Instead of Margaux, Elle saw a woman with panic in her eyes; it could have been fear. With a hood covering part of her face in the darkening evening, Elle couldn't see much more than the woman's concerned eyes. The woman squeaked out, "I need your help … now please." Without thinking, Elle grabbed the woman, ushered her inside, and pulled her to a small sofa while locking the door quickly behind her. She looked outside before locking the door and didn't see anyone else. Elle then sat down next to the woman who began to cry quietly. The woman looked desperately at Elle and asked, "Can you help me?"

Chapter 2

After quickly ushering the woman to the plush sofa in her small, waiting space of the salon, Elle offered a reassuring glance at the woman. "I need to ask a few questions, and I hope you can answer them," Elle said quietly and calmly. "Do I need to call the police?" The woman's cry softened as she shook her head no. "One more question, do I need to call a domestic hotline?" Much to Elle's relief, the woman shook her head no again. Elle was surprised at how cautious she had become since her robbery at her former salon. "I lied … one more question, are you in danger?" The woman replied again, this time with a soft "No."

Satisfied, Elle stood up from the sofa and headed toward the back room. "One good thing about opening a new salon is that I practically live here. And since I practically live here, I keep some wine in the back too." Elle poured the clearly over-twenty-one woman a glass of wine and one for herself. "I am not sure how much a hair stylist will be of assistance with what you have going on in your life, but I am happy to listen if you feel like talking. Stylists are kind of like therapists. If you don't want to talk, sip the wine until you feel better. Meanwhile, I am going to do some work and feel free to take some time to yourself." Elle started to stand up from the sofa again when the woman replied quietly, "I know you are a stylist, which is why I am here.".

Perplexed, Elle returned slowly to the sofa and clinked her wine glass to the other woman's glass. "First, cheers, and if it is a stylist you want, I am your woman. Although I have never had someone who has a hair emergency quite like this. How can I help?"

The woman pulled down her wet hood and unveiled a beautiful mane of hair, gorgeous and long. People would love to have hair like that, and Elle was trying to understand how this woman could feel like she was experiencing a hair emergency. She wasn't there to judge this woman's needs though, which was rule number one of becoming a stylist. "Do what the client wants…" Elle's thoughts returned to the woman in front of her.

Elle asked, "Do you mind if I ask your name?"

"You can call me Lucy" was the woman's reply. Elle's gut thought it was a strange response. "You can call" was clearly said by someone who was not using her real name. Elle didn't really care if "Lucy" was her real name or not; she wanted to find out more about this mystery woman. For some reason, she wanted to help this stranger in front of her and thought this woman appeared so emotionally broken; she was there for more than her hair. The two sat in silence for a few minutes, sipping their wine and sitting side by side on the small sofa.

Lucy started, "I need a change in my life. I feel like I am constantly disappointing everyone I love. Plus, I don't feel like I can trust people either. I am constantly vacillating between feeling like I disappoint people I love, or I trust the wrong people. I want a change with my hair that reveals a new me. I want to get rid of this hair that

I feel pressured to keep. It is so boring and predictable and reminds me of this pleasing life that I have continued to live. I want to be bold and need a bold hairstyle. Can you help me?" Lucy spoke this truth so fast and quickly as though she couldn't wait to get the words out of her mouth for someone to hear.

Elle felt almost guilty to take scissors to what looked like virgin hair. This woman could be a model with or without hair, as she was stunning. Elle noticed that her nails were salon-quality, and she appeared to be well-taken care of so there didn't seem to be any physical abuse that Elle could see. She wondered if Lucy had a controlling husband or a significant other, but Elle didn't see a ring either. She was so perplexed by this woman in her shop but wanted to help her. If there was anything Elle understood, that was the feeling of disappointment to the people she loved. She had been working for some time to shed that old guilt for many months, if not years, and Elle's empathy for her grew when learning just a bit more about Lucy.

"Come to my chair," Elle asked Lucy. Lucy got up and sat down in the chair as Elle began studying her hair, thinking of possible cuts. Elle noticed Lucy's heart-shaped face while draping her cape over Lucy's shoulders and continued studying Lucy for style ideas. Finally, an idea came to Elle.

"Ok, so, you want a bold new haircut, correct?" Elle talked and then ran her fingers through Lucy's long blonde hair. "Do you mind if I keep some of the length? Do you want some layers? Do you know who the rocker Nova Steel is? I am thinking of layered rocker vibes, what do you think? Are you sure you are ready for this? I hate to mention it, but the cost of the service will be $100 for the products. I am not charging you for any of my work. Women must lift up one another, and hopefully you can pay it forward, right?”

Lucy revealed the biggest smile to Elle. “We really do need to encourage one another. Thank you, Elle.”

Elle thought, *how can this woman not be a model?* She could be for all Elle knew because all she did was work. *Let's do this*, she thought to herself. “Do you need more wine? Sorry it is a bit sweeter, but I don't do a lot of sophisticated fancy wines like most New Yorkers. Do you like it?”

Lucy giggled. “It's great. Thank you.” Elle noticed a British accent emerging, but didn't know if she should say anything about her accent.

If there was anything that Elle could do after doing hair for a few years, it was talking. Elle began talking about opening up her first salon two years ago but decided to move to this neighborhood just three months ago. It cost more than what she was used to paying, but she was robbed at her old shop and decided to move shortly after the robbery. Elle mentioned that she was an only child and asked Lucy if she had any siblings.

“I have one brother. My family is complicated though. I didn't have a traditional upbringing,” Lucy shared quietly.

“I had a pretty complicated upbringing too,” Elle shared.

Both women smiled at one another. Neither one of them wanted to share much more about it, but there was something reassuring to hear someone else acknowledge family complexities, even though Elle was a thirty-year-old successful business owner.

“I am almost finished. I always like to do a blowout just to see the final effect, but it is still raining pretty hard. Are you short on time, or do you mind if I do a blowout? You look amazing already," Elle complemented Lucy.

"Sure, it would be lovely. Thank you. You have been so kind to me. I am sorry if I startled you when I arrived," Lucy confessed.

"Are you kidding? I rescue kittens from trees, help old ladies cross busy streets, and fix hair emergencies any chance I get," Elle joked.

While making eye contact through the mirror, both women smiled at each other at Elle's ridiculous effort to make a joke.

Despite being in such a weird situation, Elle thought she could be friends with this woman, even if she was holding back a bit. Elle admitted to herself, *who doesn't hold back a bit though?*

A loud knock came from the shop door, which made Elle jump.

"My driver is here," Lucy replied, looking at her phone.

"Let me help you." Elle waved the cape away from Lucy. "You look like a supermodel and Nova Steel had a baby," Elle joked again.

Both women started laughing.

Elle opened the door, and the driver welcomed himself into the small space in a somewhat pushy manner. Elle was taken aback by this entrance.

"Where have you been?" he demanded. "I am double-parked. Let's get you out of here. How much does she owe you?"

"It is $100 just for the products. I don't want any more because she was having a hair emergency, and I was here to help.   Are you the driver? Most drivers don't ask about payment. Is everything ok, Lucy?"

The driver replied, "Lucy, huh? Let's go. Thankfully, I could track you by your phone location since you went radio silent tonight."

Lucy stood up quickly and headed toward the door. Meanwhile, Elle was completely put-off by the rude driver, who interrupted Elle when he arrived as she was talking. He was so rude.

"Everything is fine," Lucy reassured Elle. "I use this driver frequently, so he knows me well and was just reminding me about the payment." Lucy gave Elle a hug and walked out of the salon quickly.

Just like that, the space seemed quiet again after Lucy left. Elle was so touched by Lucy giving her a hug. Lucy had such a presence, and Elle was a little disappointed she didn't get to know her better, but she didn't have time for too many friends; many of her old friends had lost touch with her since opening her salon.

Elle started to straighten things up, preparing to go home when she saw a small bag left by Lucy. She quickly grabbed the bag and rushed out to the car, reaching the driver's door. With an annoyed expression, the driver rolled down the window.

"Excuse me, I think Lucy left this at my shop. Here you go, Lucy." Elle tried to give the small clutch to Lucy in the back seat of the car.

"Keep it. I left it for you. You deserve more than just having me pay for the product. You created a work of art for me tonight, and it was just what I needed." Lucy's smile widened as she spoke.

The driver added, "Yeah, keep it. She always has people wanting something for nothing from her." Then the driver rolled up the
window and drove away, leaving Elle feeling crushed by the driver's
hurtful comment.

"Wait," Elle shouted to the departing car. "Jerk" she said quietly.
After Elle had such a fun, unexpected night, the driver's comment
did sting. She literally didn't charge Lucy for the work she did, so his
comment was completely off-base.

Elle's thoughts were swirling in her head. *What did he mean? Why
would people want something from her.* And based on his response to her
name, Lucy clearly wasn't her name. *Why was he so rude? Why was he
so rude to her specifically?* She was nothing but kind to Lucy.

As Elle walked back to her shop, she examined the bag that Lucy
left for her. She flipped over the bag to see a designer logo on the
outside of the small clutch bag and found a huge stack of cash inside. Elle's nervous hands began shaking as she counted the stack of
one-hundred-dollar bills. In all, she was looking at $3,000 in cash.
Lucy left a note inside: *Thanks for the rocker haircut. You are the real rock
star. Your new friend – Lucy.*

Chapter 3

The next morning, Elle was still in shock at the gift left by Lucy. She would have never accepted a gift like that knowingly from a woman in distress. She opened the shop door and dropped her enormous bag on the desk in the backroom, which still held Lucy's bag and gift. Despite being so thankful for the gesture, a pang of guilt resonated through Elle. She felt guilty for receiving money from a woman in distress. She would have never accepted a gift like that knowingly. However, even with the guilt, Elle also felt relieved that for the first time since opening her new shop, she would be able to pay herself this month and would be closer to paying off the remaining debt to her parents. Elle wonders if her parents would ever forgive her.

Elle tried to shake off her invading thoughts when Margaux came barreling through the door as usual. She always enters the room like she was being chased by someone. "You will not BEE-lieve the fun I had last night. I saw so many famous people. The movie was amazing, and everything was free for VIP guests. Do you follow *NYC Insider* on Insta?" Margaux answered her own question. "Of course you don't, you work too much. Well … I am in one of their posts from last night's event," she squealed. She started jumping up and down again.

Margaux then pulled out her phone and showed the picture to Elle. "See … that is my arm right there. Of course, my face isn't in the photo, but it's something, right? I can't believe I made one of their posts in my short time living in New York. It's a dream come true. I don't want to be famous necessarily, but just to be among the rich and famous was pretty amazing for only one night," Margaux whispered to herself more than to Elle. "To think that only a few months ago I felt stuck in my old hometown."

"Tell me about what you did last night," Elle asked, with genuine interest in the excitement that Margaux was feeling. After all, Elle felt so excited for her coworker and friend.

Margaux was shocked by her boss's new interest in her event. "Well, I went to a VIP viewing of the movie, *Echo Chamber*, as a *preferred* guest." Margaux's smile widened. "I was placed at the ropes of the entrance to see all the actors arrive for the event as well. I must admit, most of the actors were there too, except for the most popular actor. Of course, I missed them. Then, we went inside and watched the movie. There were appetizers for the VIP guests after the movie. I admit that part was a bit awkward going by myself, but it was still amazing," Margaux continued. "Thank you for showing such interest in my event. More importantly, thank you for closing for me too. How did it go?"

"It was strange. I had a woman show up here for a hair emergency shortly after you left. She was upset about something, which seemed to prompt her request for a makeover. She was actually lovely until her nosy, rude driver stopped to pick her up. Anyway, it was a good evening. I am glad you had fun. It sounds like an amazing experience." Elle smiled. "Let me see your elbow photo from the premiere; I couldn't see very well with you jumping up and down," Elle joked. "Your elbow is officially famous. When are you going to be signing auto—?" Elle stopped mid-joke as she stared at Margaux's screen. Elle looked closer at Margaux's screen and grabbed the phone from her. "Who is that guy?" Elle asked Margaux when she saw the rude driver standing among the crowd at the VIP event.

"I don't know … I think he is just someone's driver," Margaux answered, waving the question off. She continued talking about her amazing night and how she was practically on her way to New York City fame, or at least being an influencer.

"Wait! He was the rude driver last night!" Elle's voice rose in frustration while remembering their interaction. Did he do anything else there? "He walked into our shop like he owned the place. Then, he asked Lucy all kinds of questions like it was his personal business what she was doing. Finally, he insulted me as he was leaving." Elle could feel her pulse quicken just thinking about the exchange again.

"That's weird," Margaux mentions, "because most of the celebrity drivers just hang out most of the night waiting on whoever finishes with the event. Who knows, he doesn't sound very professional. Maybe he was flirting with you. Remember in middle school when boys would tease you if they were attempting to flirt?" Margaux smiled, attempting a feeble explanation for the interaction.

Both women looked at each other and laughed; Thank God they were past the middle school years. Both agreed that they would never date a guy whose charm resulted in being rude to impress a lady and began setting up the shop for the day.

Elle's first client arrived as they began their day, and she found herself in a better mood that morning. She loved thinking about the unexpected turn of events last night with meeting Lucy and couldn't believe how fortunate she felt to receive such a gift too. Her gesture was a lifesaver for her financial future. Now, how could she continue to make that kind of money every week? How can she continue paying back her parents while still investing and building her new business?

Elle refocused her thoughts on her client, asking about her client's day and how life had been since their last appointment. Elle was thankful for the handful of clients who had remained with her since her move. Elle finished with her client and began preparing her space for her next customer who would be arriving soon.

"I don't get it. These celebrities do all these promotions for their new movie and the one time I go to an event, one of my favorite celebs decides to miss it. She is still in New York, and the paparazzi are going nuts over her new look," Margaux complained.

"Speaking of new looks, you just booked a new client who is arriving in fifteen minutes. They called ahead. I'll eventually get someone to answer the phone for us, but for now we are a two-person dream team," Elle continued. "Let's get your station ready."

Although Margaux was a relatively new hire, she was so thankful for Elle who would eagerly offer her a last-minute customer who was looking for a quick cut. She did have a handful of customers but was trying to keep the few walk-in clients happy so that they may return. With that, Margaux jumped up and began to straighten up her station for her new client, who was arriving soon, and tossed her phone aside.

Elle picked up Margaux's phone and returned it to the table when a photo caught her eye. On the screen was a picture of the rude driver from last night and Lucy on the NYC Insider page; they seemed to be front and center in the photo. Lucy was really the one featured in the center of the photo as Elle examined the photo more closely. As Elle tried to read more, Margaux returned and held her hand out for her phone, thanking her boss for helping her straighten up her space for the next client. Elle's brain was reeling. Why was Lucy featured on the *NYC Insider* Insta page? Who was she?

Chapter 4

The next morning, a groggy Elle grabbed her phone and stared at the screen while staying in bed. She stabbed the phone with an angry finger and hit decline, having had all kinds of random unknown calls for the past week; she never answered those calls anyway. Elle hadn't had any extra money since opening her shop to buy whatever she assumed that person was selling anyway, she thought to herself. It was thirty more minutes until her alarm was supposed to sound but she figured she might as well get up.

"Good morning, Coco," Elle cooed to her kitty. "How are you today?" She placed his morning kibble in front of him, to which he greeted her with a rub to the leg and a very showy long stretch. Coco loved to be admired by Elle and was clearly hoping for some good morning attention. Elle gave him a quick scratch under his chin, then shuffled to the kitchen and poured herself an oat milk cold brew. She plopped herself on her sofa, and Coco quickly jumped next to her for some morning snuggles.

Elle tapped the Instagram icon on her phone, as she couldn't stop thinking about what she saw on Margaux's phone. She saw

Lucy featured on the NYC Insider Instagram page, and her brain had been trying to figure out the mystery behind it. Elle was pretty much a ghost on social media, but still glanced at it from time to time. With her family history, most of the people she knew from her past had ghosted her on social media and in life. As much as she would have liked to follow the NYC Insider page, she didn't want to invade someone else's privacy. If Lucy wanted her to know more, she would have shared it with her the night at the salon. Elle could relate to wanting to remain anonymous sometimes.

Coco approached Elle's front door and sat in anticipation. Elle asked, "Did you hear Mrs. McKinley next door?" She then opened the door to see if her sweet neighbor needed help with something and to her shock, she saw "the driver" standing hesitantly at her front door. He was standing awkwardly in front of her as though trying to decide to knock. Elle thought, what are the chances he comes to my apartment when trying to pick up someone else for a ride? Is it going to be one of those days? A random call wakes me up and the rude driver comes knocking on my door? Elle reminded herself of the not-so-great start to her day.

Elle was short with him. "I didn't order an Uber," she said and began to close the door. He held his hand out to stop her from shutting the door, and Elle was taken aback again by his behavior. She found herself standing taller, as though she was about to get pretty confrontational with this guy and was already on the defense. "By the way, I don't know if you remember me, but you were incredibly rude and suggested I was taking advantage of one of my customers just days ago, and her name was Lucy. I work very hard for everything I earn, and I don't appreciate you suggesting otherwise. And another thing, I thought you were pretty rude to her too, although I don't know your situation, but there is no need for…"

The driver interrupted her with an apology. "You are right. I am sorry. I was rude. I remember you quite well." Wait … what? Elle thought to herself. She didn't know what to say. Elle was ready to tell him what was what, and how she was completely disarmed by him being actually pleasant.

"You are right. I was completely off-base. My apologies," he stated while revealing his smile, to which she noticed his stunning smile. If Elle wasn't completely annoyed by him and still attempting to shake off the morning grog, she may have been willing to chat. In their short exchange at the shop, this was the first time she saw him. Despite being eight in the morning, he is dressed impeccably.

He had well-styled brown hair and wore a stylist button-down shirt tucked into business casual pants, not bad looking at all. He did have a bit of a charm when he wasn't being rude.

After noticing his impeccable style, Elle just realized that she was still dressed in her made-up pajamas, not even wearing real pjs but something she threw together with an old pair of shorts from her college days and a fifteen-year-old concert T-shirt. Her long brown hair was in a heatless contraption that she tried for the first time last night. She even had some spilled coffee on her shirt from yesterday morning and hadn't brushed her teeth yet.

"Oh my gosh," Elle said, feeling absolutely horrified by him seeing her like that. "I am standing in my pjs, so can I help you find someone?" Elle could no longer hide her annoyance.

"I am here to see you." Again … he smiled. That smile … now that smile was something that could charm a girl if he wasn't so annoying. Elle thought it probably worked on plenty of women, but it was too early for that.

"Please take a moment to change if you like, but I need to talk to you. I'll wait out here so we can go somewhere in a public space nearby if it makes you feel more comfortable," he continued. "By the way, I am Liam. I apologize that I didn't start with an introduction, but I am not exactly keen on my task this morning. Plus, you opened the door before I could knock," he stated, again smiling.

"Well, if you aren't 'keen' on being here, then you can leave. I couldn't possibly know why you would need to see me," Elle retorted. "By the way, how did you find out where I lived?"

"Margaux gave me your address." Liam's smile widened with his response.

That smile again. Elle could feel her cheeks reddening. Was it because she was in the world's worst pjs ensemble, or was it because this guy seemed to be flirting with her? Did she notice a slight British accent too? What is up with the British people around her lately?

"Lucy sent me to come talk to you. She said she has been trying to reach you for a few days by phone, but she must have the wrong number," he said while smiling.

Why is he smiling that charming smile again? It must work on women all the time.

"Of course, I didn't answer the phone for unknown numbers just like I don't answer my door to strange men either, regardless of how charming they may be," Elle shot back at him. Elle felt a bit guilty for that comment. She didn't know why she was so defensive with him, as she just wanted him to say what he wanted to say.

"So, you think I am charming?" He smiled again.

Elle stood there clearly not amused.

Liam was trying his best to make a better impression. "Fine. I take it that coffee is out of the question. Will you at least take my phone and FaceTime Lucy right now?" Liam held out his phone as he saw the number for "Lucy in the Sky" attempting to FaceTime Liam which he quickly hands over to Elle.

Seeing Lucy's name on the screen, Elle took his phone and slid the icon to the right and closed the door in Liam's face.

Chapter 5

After taking Liam's phone inside her apartment, Elle saw a familiar face on the screen.

"Hello Lucy!" She smiled. Elle found herself excited to see her again.

"Hello dahling," Lucy replied with a wide smile.

"Can you tell me what is going on? I am kind of freaking out right now. I have a strange guy standing outside of my apartment door giving me a phone to FaceTime a person who seems absolutely lovely, but is a complete mystery to me," Elle said without pausing to breathe. "Also, was your British accent that strong when we met because you sound really … British on FaceTime?"

"Yes, I am British, and I am in England now. I noticed when I am away from home for a lengthy period of time, my accent can change a bit," Lucy continued. "I wanted to talk to you about my hair."

Elle thought to herself, *do rich people send drivers to find their stylists when they don't like their new style? Lucy seemed absolutely thrilled with her cut, why is she calling me about it? This is such a strange conversation.*

Lucy continued, "The night I went to your salon, I was having one of the worst weeks of my life. I work in the entertainment industry, and I am in the public eye for work quite a bit. I had an avalanche of criticism that week. I trusted someone I shouldn't have trusted, despite several red flags. Then, I disappointed some people very close to me. When I visited your salon, I wanted to be a different person. I wanted to be bold and have a look that helped me become a stronger, more confident woman. You accomplished that for me. When you gave me my new look, it has been really popular in the entertainment world in which I work. It has been such a popular style; I recently had an up-and-coming fashion designer reach out to me about having their line inspired by my new look. Their show is coming up in a week, and they need a lead stylist for the show.

"As one of my requirements, I told them they had to use the stylist who gave me the look. If you are willing to take on a role for a week to be the lead stylist, the job is yours. By the way, all of your expenses will be covered, and you will be paid $50,000 for the event and potentially more if there are many presales at the show. You can build your team, or I have connections in London to help you. By the way, the show is in London. Do you like London? What do you think of my proposition?" Lucy concluded with a smile.

These British people and their adorable convincing smiles, Elle thought to herself.

Then Elle's mind began reeling about this offer. "Wait, so people like your style so much that someone created a fashion line based on your hair?"

"Yes," Lucy said while smiling. "As much as I love the designer, I told him he would have to give you some royalties from the line, regardless of whether you take the job or not."

Elle's mind begins reeling again. If Elle accepted this job, she may no longer be "off the grid" to all the people who ghosted her in her life. Was she ready for that? She had to close the shop for a week and a half to prepare and lead the show, but hopefully to see some parts of London while she was there … especially if the expenses were paid. She needed to contact a hospital while she was there to make arrangements too. Elle's mind was in a spiral with all the things to consider.

Elle didn't quite feel comfortable with leaving Margaux in charge for a week and a half. Plus, she wondered if Margaux knew who Lucy was, and Elle was sure she would want to feel included on this opportunity working for people in the "entertainment industry" as Lucy called it. With Margaux's excitement of all things Hollyweird, Elle was sure that Margaux would want to be on the style team. Not to mention, she needed to have a strong conversation with Margaux about not giving out her personal address to a random but charming stranger. As she thought of the stranger, Elle remembered that Liam was still standing in the hallway.

"Oh my gosh, I left your driver outside still. I totally forgot about him. By the way, he seemed a bit opinionated when he picked you up from my salon. Is he always that way?" Elle asked.

"He is my personal driver," Lucy said. "He is really a good guy, and I wasn't where I was supposed to be that night, which got him upset about it. He was thinking the worst about my absence. If you take my offer, he will most likely be driving you around London too," Lucy said with a smile. "I promise he is actually very pleasant normally. He is just a bit protective of people he cares about, but he is a good guy."

"I am going to get ready for work and talk to my employee. I can't make a decision without her. When do you need an answer?" Elle confirmed.

"If you can let me know by this evening , your time of course, because we have to book your transportation and make arrangements for your stay. Also, save my number, please. Toodles." Lucy ended the call.

Feeling a little guilty about making Liam stand outside for so long, Elle opened the door with a smile, handing Liam his phone.

To her surprise, Liam had five different coffees in hand and based on the logo, they came from the nearby coffee shop. Each of them had a different name written on each cup.

"I didn't know what you liked so I got five different coffees inspired by each of the members from Femme Frequency" Liam grinned slyly.

Looking slightly horrified and charmed by his gesture, Elle returned Liam's phone and took the collection of coffee. "Thank you," she said, smiled, and closed the door gently this time.

She leaned her back against the closed front door and chose the Coco Lush coffee and looked down at her coffee stained fifteen-year-old Femme Frequency concert T-shirt she was wearing from her first-ever concert with Coco Lush front and center on the design. How did he notice she was wearing this hideous, old T-shirt with their short interaction?

Elle wasn't sure the excitement she was feeling was due to her business proposition or the fact that she will get to see Liam again soon, the man who surprised her with Femme Frequency inspired-coffee, apologized for his rude behavior, and had the most captivating smile she had ever seen.

Chapter 6

After sampling each of the coffees that Liam picked up for her, Elle started making a pros-and-cons list for her business opportunity, taking a seat on her sofa near her Christmas tree. Although it was late August, she kept her Christmas tree up all year. Seeing this tree brought her so much joy, she flipped on the twinkling lights and began diving into her list. Elle was very pragmatic when it came to decision-making and rarely acted on impulsive. Once a decision was made in her mind, she moved forward full steam ahead.

Right now, there were far more pros than cons, but she still wanted to work on building her business and taking off nearly two weeks will not help win over clients. She did lose some clients with her move to the new shop because many clients just didn't want to travel that far. On the other hand, taking the opportunity meant she could pay off the debt owed to her parents; even if it did not change anything between them, it would make her feel better. With her parents' debt paid off, she would be able to really take the burden off making money, paying required bills, and growing her business. Plus, she had some marketing she would like to do and pay for some branding of products potentially. If she took the opportunity, she would have to lead a team for a fashion show, something she knows nothing about, but she did have a passion for her career and it would be such a dream opportunity. Would that be a pro or a con? She also would potentially see Liam again and figure out if he was actually flirting with her or if she was imagining it? Focus Elle, she thought to herself. This decision cannot be considered based on seeing his charming smile again. Another pro would be to see Lucy again. As strange as it seemed, Elle felt like she could be good friends with Lucy. Elle's mind was considering the different scenarios for taking the London job.

Finally, Elle started getting ready for work and texted Margaux to arrive early to work if she was available. She took one last sip of her Coco Lush coffee and admired her beautiful Christmas tree that took up far too much space in her small apartment. Feeling a solid decision come over her, Elle packed up and headed out the door.

Elle found herself walking with such purpose to work like Margaux normally would. She was ready to have that conversation with Margaux about their opportunity when she arrived at the shop and much to her surprise, she found Margaux waiting for her. Margaux looked like she had been chased to work by a crazy person. Elle looked concerned at her friend and only co-worker.

"Please don't fire me," Margaux pleaded. "I know that I am new to the job, and I asked you to close for me a few days ago, but I promise whatever I did, I am committed to doing better and to continue learning," Margaux spilled out to Elle.

"You aren't fired," Elle reassured her, "but I do have something on my mind. I do want to know why you gave the rude driver my address though."

"I didn't give him your address. He said his client wanted to give you a raving business review and asked for your first and last name; that was it. He came to your apartment? If you weren't going to fire me, you really are going to fire me now," Margaux teased with a nervous smile.

"He said I was going to get a raving review, huh? Let's have a look to see if he actually did that or if he just used the information to find my apartment. Is that even possible to find my apartment using only my name?" Elle asked herself this question.

Both women grabbed their phones and began looking up reviews.

"Oh my gosh … oh my … oh my…" Margaux was pacing.

"What? What did the review say?" Elle began to panic.

Elle Bennett, owner of Styled, is more than a stylist but she is a friend. She welcomes her clients with a warmth and confidence that quickly allows her customers to feel comfortable with her skills if it is their first or fiftieth visit. Additionally, she is a true professional. Her cut and color were not only excellent, but a trend-setting work of art that has taken the world by storm. If you want to be treated like a celebrity and a friend, go see Elle. – Skye Reynolds

Then, Margaux started crying. She was not just crying; she was sobbing. She was immersed deep in the ugly cry that prevents you from speaking or breathing. Margaux was hysterical.

"That must be an error because I haven't done hair for anyone named Skye Reynolds," Elle admitted and looking completely confused. "I appreciate that this driver took pity on my little business, but I don't want anyone giving me good reviews that I didn't earn just to drum up some business. I am not sure how to reach the driver if he was involved, but I will let him know. I did hair for a new client named Lucy, but not Skye," Elle explained.

Margaux pulled up her phone and looked at the *NYC Insider* picture of her elbow in the photo with the driver. She was sniffling now, but sniffling as she was frantically scrolling through her phone. "You know the driver that came here. This is the guy, right? The one who was rude to you the other day, right?" Margaux was determined to solve this mystery.

"Remember how I said my favorite actress wasn't at the VIP event the other night? I was so disappointed," Margaux continued. "The media has been going crazy lately because she has a new look. She always had a very sophisticated, typical, model-looking, long-haired classic look. Great actress, but her style was a lot like much of Hollywood. Well, she got a new look recently, and everyone is losing their mind over it. It's kind of edgy and a rocker-style look. She looks like such a baddie now." Margaux was giving Elle an entire history of an actress, but even Elle was beginning to make some connections with this story.

Margaux continued, "The day after the VIP event, Skye is seen around NYC with the new look. She must have gotten it here in the city and on the night of the event instead of going to the event. I know I sound like a stalker, but I saw her promoting the movie at an event earlier that day with her old look." Margaux continued to scroll through her phone while looking for something she couldn't quite find as she continued talking.

"Elle, did you do the rocker cut for Skye Reynolds?" Margaux asked while holding up her phone screen for Elle to see a picture of a familiar woman.

On the screen in front of Elle was a picture of Lucy surrounded

by paparazzi with the rocker haircut that Elle had given her just days
ago.

Chapter 7

After seeing the photo of Lucy, or Skye, whatever her name was, Elle knew that what she was going to say next may take an already emotional Margaux over the edge.

"Margaux, you need to sit down," Elle demanded.

Margaux slowly sat down on the sofa. "I need you to stay calm. Calm, calm. Got it?" Elle smiled nervously because Margaux was already so excited.

"It appears that I did give Skye her rocker haircut." Suddenly Elle heard a slow squeal similar to that of a tea kettle. Slowly, the sound seemed to become louder and was coming from Margaux who was getting teary-eyed again. "Calm, calm, remember?" Elle continued. "I have more to tell you. Grab your phone please. Will you look up to see if you can find out Lucy/Skye's real name? I just want to know, please." Elle smiled slightly while saying this.

"Even though I am a big fan, I didn't realize her birth name is Lucy," Margaux continued as she took a moment to look up information and read from her phone. Her business name is "Skye," Margaux confirmed as she was reading while staring at the screen.

"In this case, I am going to refer to her as Lucy, ok?" Elle explained. "There is more, but remember, calm. Ok? The driver, Liam, came to see me this morning. Apparently, Lucy has been trying to reach me the past few days, but I didn't know her number. I didn't know she was anyone but Lucy. She gave me a big tip, but other than that, I don't know too much about her. Well, the driver came to see me this morning and told me that Lucy had been trying to reach me. She FaceTimed me this morning using Liam's phone." Elle could hear the tea kettle sound return to the room again as Margaux was placing both hands over her mouth and eyes widened.

"Remember to be calm, ok? She offered me a business proposition. I want you to be included in this decision, ok?" Elle asked. Elle was pacing a bit as she talked, as pacing always helped her process things.

Margaux nodded quickly, pulling a blonde curl behind her ear, even if she didn't fully understand what she was agreeing to at the moment.

"Since I gave Lucy her new look, Lucy told me today that a fashion designer has been inspired by the look. Lucy's look is the muse for his new fashion line, and he needs a stylist to lead the hair and makeup for the entire show. The show is in about a week, and I need to make the decision tonight if I want to jump at the opportunity of being the lead stylist for the show." Elle stopped for a moment to process her next statement.

"I made a list of pros and cons this morning after I was offered this position." Elle sat down and went through the list of pros and cons with Margaux that she created. As excitable as Margaux could be on any day, she was more pragmatic when helping Elle make this decision. Margaux pulled out paper to make yet another list for Elle and studied the list while she and Elle brainstormed Margaux began marking out some items and circling other items on the list.

"Looking at this list, there are far more pros than cons. I think you should do it. What a great opportunity! Think of all the clients that may come here after knowing that you not only created the on-trend rocker look that is taking the world by storm, but you are leading an entire style team for a fashion show. By the way, did you say where the show will take place?" Margaux asked.

"It is in London," Elle said with a smile, still with an expression of contemplation.

"Well, there is only one thing to do and that is to pack your bags." Margaux jokingly hopped up and pretended to begin packing up Elle's things. "Ouchhhh!!!!!" Margaux yelled. "I didn't know your iron was already hot. I was trying to make a joke to help you pack your things, but oh man, that hurts!"

Elle hopped up, went to the backroom, and pulled out a bottle of something that looks like a conditioner. "Here, give me your finger." Elle then put some of the liquid on the burn.

"That feels better already! What is this stuff, and where have you been hiding it because it is not the only time I have burnt my finger on an iron," Margaux stated while smiling.

"It's in the backroom, and there are a few bottles of it. Remember how I told you that I used to like science when I was a kid? Well, I made a conditioner that has some calming qualities for sensitive skin. I learned that it works on burns too. It won't heal it, but it makes it feel better, doesn't it? I usually save it for clients with sensitive skin, but here you go; now you know about it. If you ever have a client that could benefit from it, you can use it. I have more bottles in the back," Elle mentioned.

"I couldn't be happier for you." Margaux smiled, genuinely so happy for Elle. "You deserve this opportunity. You are such a patient boss and friend. You have taught me so much in the short amount of time I have been a stylist in New York. I know you felt like you needed to close the shop while you are gone, but I think I can take care of things. If you are worried about the responsibility for me, I can work double shifts just to keep the business open during your absence. What do you think?" Margaux asked.

"What are you talking about?" Elle looked confused. "I am not thinking of closing the shop while I am gone because I am a crazy control freak and think you can't handle things. You are such a talented stylist. Yes, you are new to our work, but you are always so ready to learn. You have grown so much professionally in the time I have worked with you here. You are so amazing. I wanted to close the shop because I want you on my team for the show in London. There isn't anyone else I would trust to be my right-hand person other than you." Elle's voice was growing louder to emphasize her point. "Do you want to go to London to be on the style team for a fashion show?" Elle asked nervously.

The high-pitched tea kettle noise had returned and began to fill the room as Margaux started crying happy tears this time.

Chapter 8

After Elle and Margaux made their decision to go to London, they both FaceTimed Lucy to share the news. Elle wanted to give Margaux an opportunity to see that Lucy was just a regular person, plus Elle wanted Margaux to get past the starstruck mentality with celebrities. Elle thought of Lucy as a friend.

After making calls, lists, FaceTiming Lucy again, and making final arrangements, Elle was packing her bags. She couldn't believe how quickly things came together for this event. When she told her small, but loyal clients she had to reschedule their appointments, they were more than agreeable when they learned that their stylist was hired by Skye Reynolds. Honestly, Elle realized that this was only the second time Elle had to change appointments since starting her business. The other time she rescheduled clients was the day after her robbery, and it was understandable when she was in her old neighborhood.

Lucy gave Elle the number directly to the designer's "people," and she sent over the list of supplies she would need for the show. Since saying yes to the opportunity, Elle and Margaux brainstormed together and sketched plans for different looks for the show. They also made a list of great colors for their makeup department so that the hair and make-up would complement the designs perfectly. Although Lucy said the designer was up-and-coming, he seemed to have access to many resources, and it was amazing to Elle that she would send over a supply list that would be waiting for her upon arrival.

In the midst of making arrangements, Margaux and Elle took screenshots of ideas. Both women studied Pinterest boards for creative color combinations and looked up eighties rock icons. Margaux bought a heap of old eighties magazines from a local used books store and planned to scan through them during their flight. They packed luggage full of posters, pictures, markers, pencils, and sketches. Elle went into anything a hundred percent, and she had some ideas in mind to help the rocker look come to fruition for this show.

Elle was feeling prepared and excited for the trip too. She picked up a travel book on where locals go in London. She hoped to see the London Bridge, The Globe Theater, Buckingham Palace, and try afternoon tea during the visit. Being a Femme Frequency fan as a girl, she would love to see any memorabilia from the band. She also would love to find a cute Christmas shop with some kitschy décor from London that would be opened all year. Elle hoped that she would get an opportunity to sightsee even with an unpredictable work schedule. She couldn't believe all that had changed in her life in just a few short days.

Her cat Coco was on high-alert and didn't appreciate the fact that luggage was out and on the bed. Coco was a smart cat and knew what luggage usually meant for a cat. Elle was thankful for her great neighbor, Mrs. McKinley, who loved watching Coco and regularly checked in on the cat but brought Coco to her house to stay overnight. Elle once tried to travel with Coco, and it was a nightmare. She learned from that experience that he was happiest at home. She always left her clothes around the apartment for her fur baby to lounge around on in hopes it made him feel more comfortable during her absence.

While packing, Elle heard a knock at her door and greeted Margaux with a hug.

"Are you ready to do this?" Elle asked.

"Are you kidding me? I could hardly sleep last night! I can't believe we are doing this." Margaux's smile grew wider. "I can't believe I live in NYC, and I am going to work on a fashion show in London. I mean, who are we now anyway?" Margaux was beside herself with excitement.

With all her planning, Elle and Margaux were able to easily get through security and quickly to the plane. Margaux couldn't believe they were in first class. Elle was hopeful, but not surprised based on the connections that Lucy seemed to have that they would be treated well throughout this travel process.

As they situated themselves on the plane, Elle received a text from Lucy:

Hey dahling, I can't wait to see you. I have you both booked at an adorable boutique hotel near Buckingham Palace. I have a small surprise for you when you arrive. Yay! Liam will pick you up from the airport and has been tasked to drive you around London this week. My assistant will send you the itinerary as well. I should be able to visit you in the evening after you arrive, but you will be put to work almost immediately, meeting the Axel Scott design team. I have reservations

Elle read the message aloud to Margaux. Margaux noticed a small smile appear on Elle's face as she read Liam's name aloud.

"Who is Liam?" Margaux asked in curiosity.

"He is the rude driver," Elle replied.

"Why did you smile when you read his name?" Margaux nudged Elle with her shoulder.

"I didn't smile regarding him. I am just excited about the entire week," Elle attempted to convince Margaux.

"I think there is a bit more to the story." Margaux was convinced of that fact.

"Remember when I told you he came to my apartment to get me to answer Lucy's calls?" Elle didn't wait for an answer. "When Lucy FaceTimed me using his phone, I took his phone in my apartment and forgot he was out in the hall, honestly. He must have been out there for fifteen or twenty minutes while I was chatting away on his phone. Anyway, when I opened the door to give him his phone back, he brought me five coffees. Each coffee was named for a different Femme Frequency singer" Elle smiled remembering the memory.

"He sounds like a weirdo. What kind of grown man gets the names of the members of Femme Frequency put on his coffee?" Margaux looked completely revolted.

Elle laughed and replied, "I was wearing a fifteen-year-old Femme Frequency concert T-shirt that morning. It had a coffee stain, and I hadn't even brushed my teeth. He said when I opened the door, he didn't know what I liked, so he ordered different coffees hoping it was something I liked for coffee. It was actually kind of sweet if I wasn't completely humiliated by wearing a stained T-shirt and having morning breath. I just don't know why he would have gone to all the trouble. I have been pretty rude to him too." Elle had a tone of confession.

"He was flirting with you," Margaux teased.

"I doubt it. He was probably getting coffee for himself after I kept him waiting for so long," Elle explained. Elle started getting adjusted to sleep as the plane came to its cruising altitude. She put her mask on her forehead, requested a blanket, and put in her earbuds to help relax with soothing music.

Margaux tapped Elle's shoulder.

Elle removed her AirPod to look at Margaux.

Margaux sang quietly with a teasing smile, "If you take my hand, I will show you…" waving the photo of Liam, the driver, on her cell phone in front of Elle's face.

Elle giggled. "Goodnight," Elle whispered with a smile. Then, she changed the music to Femme Frequency and pulled her mask over her eyes with the Femme Frequency lulling her to sleep.

Chapter 9

Elle could hear muffled talking when she realized her mask was half on and off her eyes. She was really groggy; in an effort to get some sleep on the flight, and taking full advantage of the lounge seats in first class, she took some melatonin. She never took medicine, or very rarely, and she was feeling lethargic when she attempted to wake up.

Margaux tapped Elle's shoulder. "Wakey, wakey eggs and bakey. Holy cow, you look really tired. Are you ok?"

"I'll be fine. I took something to help me sleep last night and I think it is still in my system. I'll get some coffee and should liven up a bit. What was the announcement that I missed, and where is my other AirPod?" Elle, still looking very groggy, tried to look like she was much more alert.

When she couldn't find her AirPod on herself, Elle began looking down at the ground after flipping her blanket, hoping to find the tiny piece of technology.

"It's stuck to your cheek," Margaux replied and cracked up with laughter. "I have mad respect for your ability to sleep like this on an airplane and on the verge of us having an experience of a lifetime! I think I slept about twenty minutes. By the way, we are already on our initial descent." Margaux flipped open the window screen and began exploring the outside world.

Elle checked herself in the mirror and looked like she felt, but she would get moving soon. After a quick English breakfast on the flight and some surprisingly good coffee, Elle was slowly feeling better but still not quite herself.

After landing, Margaux and Elle began searching for Liam. Elle texted Lucy to let her know they had arrived and were looking for Liam. Elle's phone dinged with the shared contact for Liam. With Elle's slow, groggy fingers, Margaux took her phone to message Liam, and within moments, both women found Liam standing just outside of the hectic baggage claim exit. Elle marveled at Liam's ability to find parking just outside of the airport exit in London. She was confident that his working for someone in the entertainment industry, he knew someone who would allow for that parking without being ushered away like the rest of the world would have been.

After hopping into the car, Liam immediately noticed a change in Elle's demeanor. Liam noticed that she appeared groggy, less focused, and slow in thought. Elle admitted to taking something to help her sleep on the flight and it hadn't quite worked off yet when he asked if she was feeling ok. Liam seemed to have a sensitivity to Elle and took it upon himself to call Lucy during the drive.

"Lucy, Elle is going to need to go to the hotel to get some down time before dinner tonight. I know it's a slight change of plans but she needs some rest. I'll make sure to get her where she needs to be for dinner tonight. We will meet at the restaurant at 8:00. Goodbye." Liam hung up the phone after leaving a message for Lucy. His attention turned back to Elle.

"I changed the plans so you can get some rest this afternoon."

"You are going to too much trouble. I should be fine soon. I generally never take medicine, so I think my body is adjusting to it. I have too much to do and really don't have time to take a break. I am eager to get to work," Elle said, attempting to reassure Liam that she was just a little groggy.

"Look, I know what doing this show is going to be like. Take a couple of hours and you can work yourself crazy for the next week, but you seriously need to rest because I can tell you aren't yourself. I mean this sincerely," Liam said in a soft, concerned tone.

Elle was genuinely touched by Liam's genuine concern for her, so Elle gave up on the conversation as they pulled up to their hotel. Margaux was out of the car before Elle could make a move and would not stop talking. She couldn't tell if Liam was getting annoyed or genuinely entertained by Margaux's naïveté and child-like excitement regarding their work this week.

Elle slowly moved out of the car and it happened before she realized it. Just as she stepped outside of the car, a scooter came whizzing toward Elle. She was frozen in fear, hesitation, or just her foggy brain wouldn't allow her to move. Her feet turned to lead. She was going to get slammed by this machine within moments of arriving in London. Thankfully, it was in that moment she could feel an arm around her.

Liam's strong arm quickly surrounded her waist, pulling her to him. She could feel his warm breath on her ear, his breathing being even and controlled while Elle was reeling, and her heart was racing. Liam pulled her aside, and they were suddenly standing face to face out of harm's way on the sidewalk. Elle was no longer feeling foggy, as her entire body felt alive. Liam still had his arms around Elle in a protective manner, holding her steady until she regained herself. They were standing so close that their noses were actually touching, and there was almost an electricity between the couple as they stood facing each other, and the only thing Elle could think to do was to embrace Liam and cry.

Chapter 10

A couple of hours later, Elle came out of the shower and was finally feeling like herself. She was slightly horrified thinking about the scooter incident when they arrived at the hotel earlier that day. She was thankful to have some down time at the hotel this afternoon but humiliated by being so out of sorts in front of Liam and Margaux. It was as though she was acting like someone who had never traveled and embarrassed herself. Elle tried to busy herself while getting ready for dinner so that she would stop rehearsing what happened in her head.

It was nearly 7:15, and she was told that Liam would arrive at 7:30 to pick her and Margaux up. She is never late. Despite the dinner meeting being with Lucy, she wanted to make a good impression after this morning's debacle. Elle wanted to look smart, professional, and maybe a little pretty. Sure, Lucy may not notice that Elle looked pretty, but maybe someone else may notice. She styled her long brown hair so that it was slightly draped to one side and chose to wear a pink floral dress. She slipped on her heels, put on her earrings, sprayed perfume on, and headed toward Margaux's hotel room.

"I am so excited! I changed like twenty times for this dinner. I can't believe we are having dinner with Skye Reynolds!"

"Ok, remember calm, calm, right? She is our business partner now. She requested our expertise, and we should act accordingly, ok?"

Margaux smiled at the short pep talk and gave her boss a quick arm squeeze.

As the women approached the lobby of their hotel, Elle could see Liam standing by the car waiting for them. Liam was wearing a blue button-down shirt with black trousers with his hands in his pockets. The shirt made Liam's eyes shine. She couldn't believe he was double-parked in front of the hotel nearly fifteen minutes early, his smile widening as they approached the vehicle. Clearly, he must get special treatment too because any other person would have been shooed away from that parking spot by the parking attendant. Liam noticed her too and seemed to do a double take when he saw Elle approaching. He seemed to look her up and down, not in a creepy, invasive way, but as someone who noticed that she looked pretty and accomplished.

"Hello ladies, you both look well-rested and smart," Liam greeted both women with a welcoming smile and attempted to give Elle a hug. Elle maneuvered in an awkward side-step because she was completely caught off guard by the gesture. Elle wondered if Margaux noticed that he only offered a hug to her.

"Oh sorry, I just wanted to check to make sure you were feeling more like yourself. Sorry," Liam almost stumbled through his words, noticing that Elle was almost avoiding the hug.

"Yes, I feel a-ok," Elle replied awkwardly. Elle's words haunted her. *What am I thinking … a-ok? Why did I reject Liam's effort to give me a hug? I need to get it together!* It seemed like Liam was feeling a bit awkward too. Elle's thoughts were feeding her insecurity.

"I am dropping you off at the door. I called ahead to let them know you are arriving. The reservation is for Lucy in the Skye. The code word is "Femme Frequency." Liam's smile widened as he added the "Femme Frequency" comment.

Elle asked, "We need a code word for a restaurant?"

"You need a code word to enter the Lecture Room where you will be dining with Lucy. Due to those dining in that room, there is a code word there."

Margaux looked at Elle like all her dreams just came true.

When they entered the restaurant Sketch, Elle was in awe at the design of the restaurant. She had visited many upscale eateries as a kid, but they were old, stately, and honestly boring. The decor was a feast for your eyes there, a variety of drawings adorning the walls; Elle assumed that was why the name was chosen. Each room was decorated differently, accentuating a different art technique. Tables were not stacked on top of one another like most restaurants; instead, patrons were given plenty of space. This establishment catered to an entirely different clientele than Elle had ever seen. The patrons were trendy, stylish, and newly rich there. Elle had an overwhelming feeling of impostor syndrome but smiled at her young protege like she had all of the confidence in the world.

After following Liam's directions, Elle and Margaux entered the Lecture Room with celebrities seated at nearly every table in the space. Elle quickly grabbed Margaux's hand to help her stay grounded, terrified the tea kettle sound would soon fill the room here. They spotted Lucy, who jumped out of her chair and greeted Elle with a hug; it wasn't awkward at all. Elle and Lucy began chatting as though they were old friends. Margaux stood quietly beside both women, waiting for the cacophony of talking to end.

Margaux held out her hand to Lucy. "Hello, I am Margaux. I am Elle's associate, and it is a pleasure to meet you." Elle was absolutely dumbfounded by the confidence and maturity that Margaux exuded in that short interchange. Lucy laughed. "You divvy, I am a hugger." Before Margaux could react, Lucy pulled her in for a tight hug.

"Let's have a seat. Deacon got us the perfect table. I told him I need a bit of business and pleasure for our meeting. Do you have any allergies because I would like to get the chef's recommendations tonight? He always comes up with something that will absolutely amaze you."

Elle thought to herself that Lucy clearly visited this establishment often. "No allergies me, but Margaux can't stand mushrooms. Other than that, let's go for a culinary adventure with the chef's recommendations!" Elle said that last part with a little too much enthusiasm.

"Someone is excited about dinner," Liam teased as he approached the table behind Elle. It just registered with Elle that they did have an extra seat at the table and was surprised that he clearly was joining them.

Elle was quick with a retort. "Just watch me down the food when it arrives. Hot dog-eating champions have nothing on me!" Elle said with gusto, trying to make it appear that she was not nervous about the dinner and Liam.

Liam chortled, "Now there is the sassy girl I met in New York City. I am glad to see you are back to your old self." Both Liam and Elle allowed their looks and smiles to linger a little bit longer.

Lucy interrupted, "I want to talk a little business. First, I have been working with Axel Scott who is the designer for the show. I have negotiated an additional stipend for Margaux as your lead style assistant so that initial number I gave you will be your payment only. I also negotiated additional funds to make up for the lost wages for closing your shop for almost two weeks so that will give $15,000 for Elle and $10,000 for Margaux, which I requested in cash. I know once you begin working, it is very difficult to renegotiate any additional payment. You may also earn some additional income from sales from the show. I hope you don't mind that I negotiated a bit for you," Lucy confirmed.

"Thank you for advocating for us. You have been more than generous with your offer to look out for our best interests, even more than I could have ever imagined," Elle said, and her chin started to quiver much to her surprise. Elle was shocked by how emotional she had been today. She cried after the scooter debacle and now after Lucy showing such kindness; It was humbling. Plus, Elle hadn't felt financial freedom since leaving her parents' home years ago, and this was more than kindness. This money was giving her back some financial freedom.

After composing herself, she said, "No, thank you. Oh wait, cheers is what you Brits say for thank you, right?" Elle did her best to lighten the emotional moment or at least to hide it.

Everyone clinked glasses in a celebratory moment for this collaboration or maybe for Lucy and Margaux, it was celebrating this entire experience.

Lucy gave the women the dirt on everyone associated with this new designer. As Elle suspected, many of the designers can be a bit artsy and eccentric. Axel had an assistant little-rough-around-the-edges-chav, but an absolute charmer. Lucy suggested that Margaux get close to the assistant this week which will help everyone involved. She laid out the plans for the day tomorrow, and they would begin around ten the next morning. Unless there was a fashion show that day, typically the fashion world begins work a bit later; however, they should be prepared for very, very late nights. Europeans do work a little differently, she warned. She started late and ended late compared to Americans. Lucy also shared that she would be around throughout the week so they could sneak out for lunches from time to time. She may also be around throughout the week for some fittings because she would be in the finale of the show.

As Lucy continued sharing the plans for the week, Elle observed something unexpected. She noticed that Liam and Lucy were practically finishing each other's sentences from time to time. She also noticed that Lucy made a joke or two, and it was a hidden joke between the two of them. Clearly, he must have been driving for her for some time for them to know one another that well. Elle reconciled that Liam was invited to dinner to be aware of drop-off and pick-up times, but she thought it was odd that he seemed to know Lucy so well.

However, Elle would not allow her overactive mind to distract her from the opulence of the evening. The group feasted like royalty, and the service was absolutely impeccable. Margaux visited the restroom three times throughout the meal to secretly scope out the venue for famous people. She whispered several times in Elle's ear another celebrity name that she saw in the restaurant. Margaux was in her element with this dinner.

As they began to leave for the evening, Liam confirmed a 9:45 pick-up time for Elle and Margaux in the morning. "Actually, I have an errand to run in the morning. It is personal, so I would like you to pick up just Margaux. Don't worry, I will be there at ten promptly. I have the address from the itinerary. I'll meet everyone there," Elle announced.

Liam seemed put off by Elle's plan and a concerned crease appeared between his eyebrows.

"I am happy to get you for your errand; it is no trouble at all. It would be my honor to make sure you are where you need to be without incident." He smiled a shy smile after his last comment.

Elle smiled back. "It is personal, and I don't want to waste your time. Thank you though. Thank you for driving us again. Lucy, you are the best. Thank you so much for everything, and I can't wait to hang out this week despite our busy schedules. I hope you don't mind, but I kind of consider you a friend, not just a coworker," Elle admitted.

"You are the rock star, not me, remember?" Lucy smiled that celebrity smile as they said their goodbyes at the restaurant.

Liam pulled up to the front of the hotel, and Elle and Margaux grabbed their things to leave. Lucy said something inaudible to Liam and both laughed at her comment. That's when Elle finally put her finger on what she couldn't place at dinner, wondering if Lucy and Liam were actually more than friends because clearly, they

have some chemistry.   With that, Elle slowly closed the car door,
waved goodbye, and entered the hotel lobby with these thoughts,
second-guessing anything she thought she had with Liam.

Chapter 11

Elle woke up early to allow time to visit the hospital before her first day of work at the fashion house. Margaux promised to bring the vision boards to the fashion house because Liam would be able to help transport her with all of the supplies. Elle also considered this small task a "test" to see if Margaux could remember to bring all of the materials and to keep them organized as well. She would be relying on Margaux all week so she wanted to make sure Margaux was up for the task.

Elle put on her tennis shoes because she was walking a few blocks, but she was also excited to take in the sights and sounds of the city during her walk. Heading out of the lobby, she put in one of her AirPods so that she could hear the directions from maps without looking like a complete tourist. She grabbed a coffee from a cafe just steps away from the hotel. *Ahhh …* Elle thought to herself, *this would be so amazing to experience this life here every day.* Despite loving New York City, the atmosphere there in London was historic but also urban. It also seemed a bit "welcoming" by the friendly nods as Elle walked the city streets and spent the evening there yesterday. Elle did realize that she had only been experiencing the city for less than one day so she may have been romanticizing her first impression a bit. However, Elle was thankful that she was not experiencing any jet lag and was ready for the day today.

Before realizing it, Elle was already approaching the hospital. She texted her friend to confirm her location before attempting to navigate the sprawling campus of St. Thomas Hospital. Of course, her friend Prina was able to land a residency there at St. Thomas Hospital in London. She was a phenomenal student and always set her mind to her goals.

As Elle rounded the corner, in the hopeful direction of Prina, she heard, "If you take my hand...," and Elle turned on her heel and saw a dear friend. Elle answered, "I will show you…" and both friends embraced and laughed.

"You haven't changed a bit, Dr. Patel," Elle greeted her old friend. "Or do I hear that your last name may be changing soon?"

"You haven't changed a bit either, and you are already asking about my love life," Prina Patel said and smiled back. "You are correct though … I am officially engaged. Despite all the pressure from my family to accept help from my auntie to find a man, I found the love of my life and I don't mean work." Prina was beaming.

Elle was absolutely shocked to see a softer side of Prina. She was always so focused on her goals and work so Elle was thrilled to see her friend find some balance in her life. She always pushed herself so much, and her parents were much like Elle's family, expected excellence.

"I didn't get to tell you too much of my reason for my visit to London. I am working for Axel Scott, who is an up-and-coming fashion designer. He hired me because I gave someone famous, who

I didn't know was famous, a new haircut, and it has been a bit popular, so I was offered a job as the lead stylist," Elle said casually.

"You act like you gave Skye Reynolds her new cut. The paparazzi have been losing their minds lately about her new look," Prina laughed.

Elle smiled a sheepish grin.

Prina's eyes widened, and her mouth dropped open in disbelief. "You are not bloody kidding, are you?" Prina's voice was almost a whisper.

"Actually, yes, I did give her the new style. It is an amazing opportunity because I am able to finish paying back my parents, and now I can look into developing the material that I sent you."

From Elle's tone, Prina could tell Elle was not in the mood to discuss her parents.

"Tell me about what you have done with the samples that I sent you," Elle smiled.

"I divided the samples you sent me and sent them to several more colleagues who are doing medical research in my field. They have conducted some studies, and the findings are quite promising. How long are you going to be in town? After I received your text, I wanted to gather more information from my colleagues since you were in town. I can gather the formal documentation from everyone and meet with you outside of work sometime this week. Let's coordinate. I think you will have most of what you need to move forward," Prina encouraged Elle.

"That's fantastic. I'll be in touch this week to schedule our dinner. If you want, we can meet at a cafe to talk about the studies and then have a nice dinner together. I would love to meet your fiancé."

"I would love for you to meet him too, and he has a very single best friend who is absolutely gorgeous, kind, and smart. He is studying to be a pediatrician of all things. How adorable is that? What do you think about meeting him too?"

Elle smiled at her dear friend. "It sounds like fun. I am busy this week, but I can always make time for you."

"I have to go. I don't want to be late for my first day," Elle leaned in for a hug from her former college roommate and dear friend, despite all of the ups and downs of Elle's life in the past few years.

"By the way, if the data continues to look good, you need to think of a name for this venture," Prina suggested with a wide smile.

As Elle walked away from her old friend, she attempted one of their old routines as roommates, turning around slowly in a dance-inspired maneuver while reaching out her hand dramatically to Prina… "If you take my hand…" Ella continued her moves outside the sliding doors of the hospital.

Prina responded, "I will show you…," while mimicking Elle's dramatic moves.

Both women rolled with laughter.

Elle stepped out of the hospital lobby still humming the Femme Frequency song that she and Prina used to belt out in their younger years. She put in her one AirPod again to hear the directions and realized that she would have time to go back to the hotel and ride with Margaux. Little did she know, she walked past Liam, who had followed her to the hospital and was sitting discreetly on a bench watching Elle leave.

Chapter 12

Elle texted Margaux to let her know she was on her way back to the hotel. She felt a pang of guilt about not sharing the product project with Margaux because she really considered her a friend, not just a colleague. Eventually, Elle would tell Margaux about her little project, but for now, it was easier to keep it private to see if anything even came of it.

She could see the hotel from a distance and knew she could sense something. After getting robbed in New York City a few months ago at her shop, Elle had been even more aware of her surroundings. Being a city girl most of her life, she was always aware, but the robbery had made her a bit unsure of herself at times. And then, she felt a hand touch her shoulder.

Elle whipped around quickly while simultaneously making a karate chop move with her left hand in front of her body. She had no idea what she was doing with that weak attempt at self-defense and was shocked when she saw a familiar face in front of her.

"What were you doing at the hospital? Did you have an appointment to get pain medication or something? I don't want Lucy around that influence." Liam was practically interrogating her.

Elle was shocked. "How did you know I was at the hospital? Did you follow me?" Elle was furious. She didn't know if he was a driver and some kind of bodyguard. Maybe he was just Lucy's jealous lover, she wondered. "Seriously, did you follow me?" Elle insisted this time, and her anger was palpable.

"Of course I followed you. I needed to know what your errand was because I need to make sure you are not only supposed to be where you are supposed to be today, BUT I also wanted to make sure you weren't doing something suspicious because Lucy doesn't need to be around anyone like that," Liam said quickly without stopping for a breath. He was acting very protective of Lucy; Elle didn't know what to make of this interaction.

"What are you talking about? People can't go to a hospital unless they're some kind of addict in your eyes? Is this your way of asking me if I feel ok too? What the heck? Why can't you give me any credit for being a decent human being?" Elle was on a roll at this point. "Plus, you insulted me the first time we met about wanting something from Lucy like I am some kind of manipulator. You do realize that Lucy actually came to my business that night? I didn't find her! I thought we were past this judgy thing you had going at first with me." Elle was ready for this argument with Liam. She was seething.

Liam's eyes fell. "You are right. I was off base with my questioning, but I did want to make sure you made it to the fashion house today on time. Lucy has had a history of working with some flakey people, and I wanted to make sure that you were the real deal. I mean, you seem like a great person, but I just didn't know. By the way, you didn't really answer my question about what you were doing at the hospital," Liam persisted. He was not afraid to offend Elle at all in an effort to protect Lucy.

"I went to see a friend from college," Elle nearly said the words through gritted teeth. "I had to make time to see her when I could, which was before work today. That is the only time I have today, at least as far as I know. I imagine I won't be back at the hotel until late tonight. Literally, this was the only time I had today," Elle said again with words so distinctly pronounced that each word was emphasized at the end of her sentence. She was nearly spitting the words at him through gritted teeth. Elle emphasized that her actions were actually the complete opposite of what an irresponsible person would do, but someone who actually took their job seriously.

"I am sorry. I feel like I have spent most of my time apologizing to you. You are right. I shouldn't have come at you so aggressively, but Lucy has a knack for trusting the wrong people. Did Lucy tell you what happened to her the night she showed up at your shop? Did she tell you why I was so angry with her about it?" Liam asked but appeared to be explaining his actions through his questions too.

Elle looked confused. "No, she didn't tell me details, but she told me she needed something bold and that she wanted to be a bolder person. She said she disappoints people around her all the time. Lucy said that she trusts the wrong people too. So no, I guess I don't know what happened."

"Well, it isn't my story to tell. Lucy really likes you, and I am sure she will tell you when she is ready. That story may provide some clarity on why I was so defensive this morning. I do apologize for offending you," Liam said earnestly.

"I am glad we cleared things up, but I can promise you that I am not a lunatic, druggie, scoundrel, rascal, or head-case. I am a workaholic who is trying to build my business. I want to get better at what I do for my career, be a good human being, and stay true to my faith. So, does that give you more insight on me?

"Let me know a bit more about you. One thing is true is that I know nothing about you. How long have you been a driver? Have you always done that?"

Elle wanted to get to know him better because if they were working together this week, she didn't have the capacity to defend herself every time she did something he didn't understand. Plus, she was too busy building a show this week and didn't have time for this nonsense. Instead, she tried to be patient to understand him and get to know him where this protective driver bit regarding Lucy came from.

At this point, both Elle and Liam were walking inside the hotel lobby.

"I started to drive for Lucy about two years ago when I saw that she needed someone to not only drive for her, but to also look out for her." Liam began to open up about their connection.

"One more question, how long have you and Lucy been a thing?"

Liam looked completely confused. "What are you talking about?

"You guys were nearly finishing each other's sentences last night. You clearly are closer than just acquaintances. You practically came at me this morning because you thought I would be a bad influence on Lucy. How long have you guys been a thing?" Elle was persistent because she didn't want to deal with a jilted or jealous man looking over her shoulder this week.

"You really don't know much about the entertainment industry, do you?" Liam found her comment almost comical that she was the one person in the world who didn't realize their connection. "Lucy is my sister," Liam smiled.

Elle nearly stopped in her tracks after hearing Liam and Lucy were brother and sister. Her heart was pounding, and she felt a little flutter in the pit of her stomach. Elle was still completely irritated with him for being so accusatory this morning, but then again, she wished that she had a brother who was protective like this too. Elle had a bit of sympathy for him trying to protect his sister, especially after knowing something must have happened the night she met Lucy. Elle did understand why he may have been so skeptical about her.

"So, when are you going to show me some of your karate moves?" Liam teased, "because I really feared for my life when you tried that maneuver on me moments ago. I mean … business owner, hair stylist, and sensei. How do you find the time, Elle?" Liam's eyes twinkled when he was teasing.

Now, this guy flirting and joking was someone Elle would like to know better.

Chapter 13

Elle hoped that Liam didn't notice her hopeful reaction to hearing that he and Lucy were brother and sister. Despite him being so rude to her again and following her to the hospital, she believed his heart was in the right place. Admittedly, Elle would probably confront someone if she felt Margaux was at risk of getting taken advantage of or manipulated. With a bit more pep in her step than just moments before, thinking about the prospect of getting to know Liam more, she saw Margaux approaching her with hands full of the supplies for the day's work.

"Hey girl, I was able to finish my errand a little early. Do you need a hand?" Elle walked up and took some items off of the very large stack of supplies that Margaux was attempting to carry to Liam's car without realizing that Margaux and Liam had just had an argument. As far as Margaux was concerned, their day was just beginning.

"I think I need ten hands."

Liam also offered to help carry all of the vision boards that Elle and Margaux created for each of the designs that Axel Scott's team sent her. She was hoping that everyone was impressed with her ideas when they arrive.

"These are really impressive, ladies. I have never seen anyone so prepared for a meeting that involves my sister," Liam added.

"Who is your sister?" Margaux inquired.

"Lucy is my sister. How are you two just figuring this out before now? I figured you could tell because we kind of look alike and we completely mess with each other all the time. You know a goofy brother and sister kind of thing?" Liam asked, waiting for an "aha" moment to hit Margaux.

"Ohhhhh … That makes so much sense now," Margaux confessed. She moved her eyebrows up and down at Elle, as though she was giving her some hidden messages that Elle should go for it with Liam. Margaux could tell there was some interest on Elle's part toward him.

"We are just a short drive from the fashion house, so don't worry about being late," Liam reassured the team, as though he already knew their nerves were kicking in for each of them.

As promised, Liam pulled up to the Axel Scott Designs headquarters in what seemed like minutes. There was nothing subtle about the outside of the building. If he was up and coming with his work, they couldn't imagine how nice a highly successful designer's place could be.

Despite having an old exterior, the paint on the building was a cross between graffiti and a Monet painting, abstract and beautiful at the same time. His logo suited the rocker style perfectly; Elle wondered if that logo was designed specifically for this show. She believed that the event would happen here in this building later that week based on what she had been told by Lucy.

Elle requested that easels be delivered so that she could place each of the vision boards for the looks he hoped to achieve within view of the team. On each board was a print-out of each outfit, with suggestions for not only make-colors but also photos of famous rockers who had ideal makeup for inspiration for the makeup artists. Additionally, Elle sketched ideas for hairstyles for each outfit.

"Oy … oy! Come in here!" A short, but chav-looking person called Elle into the building. "My name is Callum Jones, and I am Axel's right-hand man. Welcome to the Axel Scott Fashion House." Callum held out his hand to formally greet the women.

Margaux and Elle brought in their vision boards with Liam's help.

"I'll be leaving so that you can get to work. I am just a text away. If you need some food or something, let me know. Text when you are ready to head back to the hotel. I am here for you," Liam said and offered his charming smile again.

His last words seemed to be directed right at Elle, as he wasn't looking at anyone else when saying, "I am here for you." Elle's heart was pounding, and she felt like her face was a bit flushed. She hoped that no one noticed.

"Thank you so much. You have been," Elle paused, "quite the wonder." Elle returned a secretive smile to Liam. "I'll be in touch." Elle knew that Liam understood her comment and was teasing him about earlier today.

"Callum, I am planning to set up the vision boards. When do you expect Axel to arrive? I have been told that start and end times at work may be a bit different than what I am used to, so I want to make sure I am ready when he arrives."

"You are the bloody best. I am not sure Axel has ever seen someone quite this prepared for work. Ok mate, he arrives around 10:30. He is going to be chuffed about your planning. So, get it set up, but be flexible with his feedback. He is a demanding bloke, but he knows what he is doing. It can be a chock-a-block here as we get close to show day, but your plans are going to go over very well. Have at it and I'll be back at 10:20."

"Thank you so much. We appreciate the help and insight," Elle mentioned.

"I love your style. Sorry, I just had to tell you before we get to work," Margaux gushed as she complimented Callum.

"Cheers," he said over his shoulder as he was walking out of the room.

Elle and Margaux set to work with Elle advising the makeup team but instructing the hair team. All the designs were inspired by the work of Axel Scott. Owning her own business gave Elle insight to make sure that the designs were front and center in the vision boards. She wanted to make sure that Axel felt like his work was celebrated on each design. The ladies were making quick work of it. Elle was so pleased with how easily the two worked together and that Margaux passed the test this morning with flying colors. They set up their last board and set the easels around the perimeter of the room. Both women took a deep breath as they were thankful, they set up everything. This dream was getting real, then they heard someone enter the room.

"Hellooooo dahlings, who is ready to rock the fashion world?"

Both Elle and Margaux turned to see who must be the fashion icon, Axel Scott.

Chapter 14

"**Y**ou must be our highly recommended team that Skye raves about. Let's see what we have here. It looks like someone has been doing some homework," Axel cooed. He walked through the room with all of the easels setup and examined each one of them closely. He didn't introduce himself and went from one board to another, standing in front of each one for some time. He exuded the presence of royalty.

Elle was getting restless, not sure if she should introduce herself to Axel Scott or just pretend, they don't need pleasantries to do work together. Elle walked up behind Axel and stood a few feet away from him, but close enough to hear him talking to himself about the board display.

"Why did she put so many options for the makeup recommendation for this piece? This is my showstopper design. The is ending our show with Skye wearing it, so we need more clarity for the team putting it together." He was still talking to himself. He took out a Sharpie and began marking all over the beautiful boards that Elle designed. Her heart sank. She and Margaux worked so hard on these vision boards, and he was tearing them apart with a big black

Sharpie.

Elle couldn't stay silent any longer.

"So, we created this combination of color to allow the makeup artist the autonomy to decide which would highlight the features of the model while enhancing your designs. We didn't want to continue with a steadfast color palette if it didn't complement the model and the outfit." Elle stood closer behind him, making an effort to be assertive while trying not to come off too pushy.

Axel still didn't engage in a conversation with Elle, not even turning in her direction. He continued to study the designs on the boards that encircled the perimeter of the room, working his way around the room and writing all over the boards. He was circling some things while putting a large X over other things on the boards.

Elle was distraught, wringing her hands but immediately stopped once she realized what she was doing. Elle didn't take criticism well but didn't want Margaux to see her feeling anxious and knowing that she was feeling like a failure based on the awkward reception and watching Axel nearly stabbing her boards with his Sharpie. After remembering Margaux was also watching this as well, Elle walked to her protege and took her hand, giving it a reassuring squeeze. She then gave Margaux a reassuring smile like she was completely prepared for this type of thing when dealing with designers. Elle pretended that she was feeling confident and not riddled with anxiety during their strange interaction with the designer.

After making his way around each of the boards, Axel started toward the door. Still, he didn't say anything directly to anyone other than himself.

Elle found herself opening her mouth, but nothing came out. She was caught completely off guard with this interaction or lack thereof, expecting an eccentric debutante but not a diva.

Elle again grabbed Margaux's hand, and the two of them walked slowly around the room to interpret the different markings provided by the designer. Clearly, it looked like some form of feedback, but some of the comments were a bit unclear. The markings reminded Elle of her old college days with the professor's marks on her lengthy essays, which she was used to being criticized due to the competition and demands of the program.

Both women were startled when Callum appeared in the room. "Well, well, well, ladies, it sounds like you made quite the impression on Axel Scott."

Elle questioned, "Is that a compliment?"

"You were able to capture Axel's vision for this show. He wants you to create new boards and remove the sections with X's and keep the items circled. He feels that you are giving the stylists too many options. Rather than this or that, choose the color combination that the makeup artists will use. He loved the idea of the boards and has never had a lead stylist have such vision for planning. He is now making it a requirement for his future shows. Now, get to work redesigning the boards. Axel is bringing in the hair stylists tomorrow so that they will see the new boards first and begin practicing the hair with the models. The following day, we will have the makeup team. The third day will be our dress rehearsal for the show and the fourth day is the show. Any questions?"

"Will Axel Scott actually talk to us eventually?" Margaux asked with hopeful anticipation.

"Oh dahling, he will, but he never knows how one will react when getting feedback from a visionary. Some of the lead stylists cry, and he doesn't deal with tears. Plus, he doesn't waste his time with anyone other than professionals, so prove yourself and you will have a very valuable ally," Callum said confidently, revealing the respect he has for the stylist.

"Well, you don't have to worry about that with us." Elle felt the need to prove herself again. Thinking quickly, she wanted to show Callum she was a professional. Turning to Callum, she said, "Here is what I need: a Bluetooth speaker, more coffee, lunch delivered around 2:00, metal baking sheets, purple, red, black, white, and gold spray paint, glue guns, magnets, a drop cloth for paint, and colored pencils."

"Okay, Queen. It looks like someone is here to disrupt the fashion world with us. You will have the supplies within the hour." With that, Callum left the room.

Elle turned to Margaux. "It sounds like our designs were a success but need to be clearer for the stylists tomorrow. Will you text Liam and let him know we will be late tonight, and we can Uber back to the hotel?"

"Got it. Though I don't have Liam's number," Margaux pointed out to Elle.

"Oh here. Just use my phone." Elle handed her phone to Margaux while she started grabbing the boards.

"Sure, no problem. But why is our super-cute, totally eligible driver texting you to tell you are going to 'crush it' today?" Margaux's smile widened because she thought she might have already known the answer to that question.

Chapter 15

Callum was absolutely correct that the supplies would arrive within an hour. It was almost noon, and Elle could already feel that she needed more coffee, but she didn't have time to go out. She had too much to do.

"We need some good music to get in our zone, so what do we want to hear?" Elle asked Margaux.

"We need some rock to help us get in the zone for sure, so I made us a playlist," Margaux said with excitement.

"Of course you did," Elle shouted over her shoulder as she put drop cloths for the paint on the floor.

Both women heard a gentle knock from the door of their workspace in the fashion house.

"Who would be knocking because everyone so far has been kind of loud and pushy?" Margaux whispered to Elle as she approached the door. "Well … except for the actual designer who wouldn't stoop to speaking to the hired help," she joked.

When Margaux jumped up for the door, she found Liam standing there holding three cups of coffee in a container.

"You are reading my mind. Pleaseeeeee tell me the coffee is for us. Please! I am already feeling the need for more caffeine, and you are my hero. Literally, you saved my life dodging a scooter, and now you saved my life by supplying me with more caffeine," Elle joked. Elle practically begged for the coffee in Liam's hands by reaching with outstretched arms and doing "gimme hands" like a toddler. She didn't care what it was, just as long as it was caffeinated.

"Why, yes, it is. Margaux texted me that you are working late tonight so I decided to bring some liquid energy for you. Margaux sent me her order, but I think I remembered your favorite item the last time I bought you coffee." His smile growing wider. Liam seemed to enjoy being the person to bring Elle coffee; honestly, Elle didn't mind him bringing her coffee either.

Elle took the cup from him. Again, Coco Lush was written on the side of the cup. Elle's smile widened so much that it reached her eyes with reading the name. She looked over at Margaux, feeling a little self-conscious of the obvious flirting, and Margaux was watching and smiling from ear to ear.

"So, can I lend a hand? I have about an hour and a half to kill before I need to run another errand. How can my inexperienced hands help?" Liam waved his hands in the air like jazz hands.

"Actually, you can help spray-paint this metal pieces with different colors. We have drop cloths down to help reduce any mess. It would be great if you could help with that. Actually, can you find a garden area to spray? I think this will dry faster in the sun," Margaux asked. Elle knew Margaux well enough that she had an ulterior motive to roping Liam in helping.

"Now, this is a job I can do." Liam grabbed the supplies and went outside in search of a space to do the work.

"Wow, Miss Bossypants putting our driver to work," Elle teased Margaux.

"Please, you and I both know there is a little thing between the two of you. He used this as an excuse to come spend time with you. Elle and Liam sitting in a tree…," Margaux started to sing.

"You are such a little matchmaker, aren't you? Let's get to work on pulling off each of these pictures on the boards. We need to put magnets on the backs of the photos we are keeping. I am thankful we laminated Axel's design photos. I have also brought some extra photos that I want to add. So here is the plan: We are going to put the photos that are kept on the baking sheets using the magnets on the back. Axel can move things around instead of us starting from scratch if he wants to make any further changes. I am also adding more options on an extra board in the event Axel wants to change or add more ideas to finalize his vision. Does that make sense?"

"You are a rock star, Elle. I am so thankful you brought me here. I am learning so much from you, and this is a great idea, so we don't have to reinvent our work tomorrow if Axel goes crazy with a Sharpie again. Remind me to hide all the Sharpies in the building tomorrow before he arrives," Margaux jokes.

After nearly two hours of work, Liam returned. "I have to go get your lunches. So, what do you want? Elle, I know you mentioned ordering some Indian food during your visit when we went to dinner, so do you want me to pick up some Indian food for you?"

"You are going to get our lunches too? I feel terrible putting you out of your way like that. You are the driver, but I feel like we have you doing multiple jobs for us this week: lifesaver, driver, assistant, and all-around good guy," Elle complimented Liam.

"I would like sandwiches," Margaux requested. "Any sandwich with lots of meat."

"In that case, I'll take a veggie sandwich. I am not picky; I'll eat anything," Elle explained. "Are you sure I can't pay for it?"

"Honestly, I enjoy doing things for you," Liam said with a smile. He paused as if he wanted that last sentence to sink in. "It is no bother at all," Liam replied after a second. Both Liam and Elle stood there looking at each other after he said those words. His honesty made Elle's heart race and her face turned warm. She was wondering if her hands were shaking because of the coffee or because she was fighting the urge to pull Liam closer to her.

"Thank you so much. I don't know how much Lucy is paying you, but she should pay you double this week." Elle tried her best to lighten the moment, even though she could have stayed right in that spot and looked at Liam for much longer.

"Like I said, it is an honor to help you." With those words, Liam left the room with promises to return soon with some food.

Elle and Margaux continued to dig into their work and picked up the painted baking sheets in the back of the building that Liam completed. They had magnets on each of the photos and the additional options that Elle felt obligated to prepare for just in case Axel needed them the next day. As Elle looked at their efforts, she was surprised that they may not be there as late as she thought.

"Margaux, I think we only have about two more hours of work

honestly. After we get the boards ready, you are welcome to go back to the hotel if you like. Do you have any places you want to visit while we're in London?" Elle asked but was quickly interrupted by Liam returning with lunch.

"Our hero!" Margaux cheered.

Liam put down a blanket in the room and set out three different sandwiches. He brought out the drinks and put a little centerpiece on the cloth that had small flowers in it. It was an adorable set-up. Elle couldn't help but notice the extra effort that he seemed to put into bringing lunch.

"Liam," Margaux continues, "I am impressed with this set-up. So, do you have side gigs as an assistant, picnic aficionado, driver, lifesaver, and all-around dreamy guy? I mean, how are you not already in a relationship because you are quite a catch," Margaux cooed. Although she was talking to Liam, Margaux was looking at Elle to see her reaction. Elle's eyes widened with Margaux's teasing.

"Ok ladies, I hope you don't mind, but I am joining you for lunch today. I am sure you won't have time like this for the next few days, so I wanted to take advantage of your downtime." Liam was so encouraging.

Elle was so thankful for the lunch and the gesture of a picnic lunch indoors. In true London fashion, it began raining that afternoon, and an indoor picnic was perfect. With Margaux present, the conversation was lively and light. They joked and talked about London. Liam was offering an education on London slang terms when Callum arrived to join in on the conversation.

"Hello geezers and birds, sorry to crash your party, but I need to get an update on your work. I need to have an even happier Axel tomorrow," Callum explained.

Elle and Margaux updated Callum on their work, and he was genuinely impressed with their vision too. Surprisingly, Callum was a bit serious this time and commended both women on their work. "Axel is going to be quite pleased. Thank you. You've made my job quite easy. Now, I can actually go out with some friends tonight and get properly pissed."

Elle wasn't quite sure if Callum was being serious about his plans. She would never jeopardize the chance of arriving late on such an important day like tomorrow.

"Margaux, I hear that you love to go places and have some fun experiences. Do you want to come and meet some proper Essex blokes? I am going out with my mates from primary school. They are a bunch of fun Charlies, but you will come to a British knees up?" Callum asked.

"Are you kidding me? I would love to go out and meet some of your friends. It sounds like a blast. At least, I think that is what you just asked me to do," Margaux joked.

"Don't worry, gramps. I'll make sure she gets back safe and sound to the hotel," Callum teased Liam.

Liam had a serious look on his face as he watched Margaux and Callum exchange Snaps.

"I'll see you tonight, Margaux," Callum shouted over this shoulder as he left the room.

"Margaux, Essex blokes are pretty wild and are known to do really stupid stuff. It sounds like you are going out in a nice area, so I feel better about that, but you need to be safe. I am giving you my contact information as well. I want to take you, and I am happy to come back to pick you up. Don't let any of them buy you a drink that you don't see getting poured yourself. I don't think Callum would allow something to happen, but I don't know about his Essex friends either." Liam sounded more like her dad than a thirty-year-old man. Elle's heart warmed even more toward Liam after she heard his advice to Margaux. She was beginning to understand how protective Liam was with people he cared about or felt responsibility for.

Elle was beginning to understand his defensiveness when his sister ended up missing and in her salon the night she met him. "Ladies, I am going to leave so message me when you are ready to get picked up tonight." Liam then started cleaning up the remnants of the picnic.

Two hours flew by, and Margaux and Elle finished their work. "Go ahead and leave if you like. I heard Callum offered you a ride to the hotel to get ready. I am going to finish up just a bit more. Just text Liam to let him know that you don't need a ride to the hotel. Give me a hug and please be safe tonight, ok?"

Elle continued her work after Margaux left and realized how late it was based on her stomach growling again. She finished up the work and texted Liam to let him know she was ready to be picked up when he was available.

"I am parked out front. I thought you would finish up soon, so I came a bit early. Come outside when you are ready."

Elle placed all the new boards in their spots for tomorrow. She looked back at the room with a little pride. Whatever Axel's reaction was tomorrow, she was proud of the work she had done today. Elle knew not to rely on the approval of someone else, because she knew she and Margaux did some great work that day.

She arrived outside to see Liam leaning against the car with the door propped open for her.

"Your chariot awaits. You must be hungry again."

"I am starving actually."

"Well, I have the perfect, little place in mind for a quick bite before we get to your hotel. It won't take long because I know you must be exhausted." Liam looked into the rear view mirror; again, their eyes lingered on each other for far too long. The connection between the two of them was palpable.

"That sounds lovely," Elle said with a smile.

"First, I have a surprise for you," Liam almost whispered.

Chapter 16

Just being near Liam and the fact that he planned something just for her made Elle's heart race. Liam pulled up to a shady, rather empty road and stopped the car. Elle was a bit hesitant about being surprised by someone she was intrigued by but didn't honestly know much about him yet. Her heart sank as they pulled up to the dimly lit area with very few people on the street. She did see a handful of twenty-somethings walking together from a distance, which brought her some reassurance of her safety.

"We are here." Liam grinned, clearly trying to impress Elle.

"We are where, exactly?" Elle's question sounding a bit sterner than what she meant to sound like, but she had trouble hiding her concern.

"Come on. I think you will like it." Liam smiled again with that charming beautiful smile and opened the door to the car. "Do you want to join me?" Again, that smile that made Elle's stomach drop.

"Did you just quote an animated feature?"

"Did you just notice that I quoted an iconic children's movie? Are you a fan of Starlight Studios movies?" Liam teased.

"If you mean a 'Starlight Studios fan' as someone who loves watching completely predictable animated features with complex characters who struggle with self-worth and identity while attempting to do their best in the big wide world? Then, yes, I am a Starlight Studios fan. Although, I do have to say that *Reginald the Enchanted* was one of my favorite love interests. I, mean, who doesn't love a lowly servant pretending to be royalty only to steal the heart of a princess?" Elle deadpanned.

"So, you are telling me that you would like to find yourself a lowly servant or a lowly driver?" Liam retorted.

"Of course, unless he is rude to me on several occasions, then that is a no-go."

"Well, hopefully he can show you the error of his ways and he will hopefully have the chance to make it up to you. I hope I brought you to the right place that might impress you just a bit."

Elle noticed that Liam had taken her to the entrance to a series of very old brick steps leading down to a dark space that she believed she could hear a low hum of indistinguishable noise. Liam held out his hand and guided Elle down his steps.

"Mind your step here." Liam held out his hand and took the steps ahead of her to make sure she found her footing.

Although it was dark, Elle stepped down onto a cobblestone path. The lighting was very dark, but the space was illuminated by torches that gave the area a beautiful charm.

"This place is stunning, actually. Where are we?" Elle was confused but intrigued by the space before her.

"We are at one of my favorite places for food trucks. I happened to take note that you don't eat meat very often, and this little place offers some great vegetarian options. Plus, there is a little view of the Thames River. There is also a band called Jazz Rats who play around here from time to time. Is this ok? I thought you would be starving by the end of your day. Is this ok?" Suddenly Liam's uncertainty was showing, and he appeared a bit nervous.

Elle could tell that Liam appeared to be a bit anxious with his effort to impress her. She loved that he was taking such care to plan such a thoughtful venture; honestly, she was taken aback by his gesture. It was true that she rarely ate meat and he actually noticed it. Her last boyfriend didn't realize until four months into their relationship that she had two piercings on her left ear only. Liam noticed the small details and recognized that Elle would be starving after her busy day too. She was beginning to be impressed by him as she was getting to know him better. Liam was so attentive and she really enjoyed it, even if she wouldn't consider herself someone who wanted much attention.

"It's lovely," Elle practically whispered. "Thank you. This is such a nice surprise. Really, thank you." Elle was so accustomed to being in charge that she rarely had someone take care of her like this.

"Don't get too excited because we are ordering from a food stand and most likely will be sitting on a curb or bench to dine." Liam grinned sheepishly. He seemed nervous about how Elle would react to the "surprise."

"It's really perfect. I love the ambiance of this place. I love how it looks like mostly locals come here and how the torches illuminate the area. Plus, the view of the Thames is stunning. Thank you,"

Elle said genuinely, and she felt true appreciation of all that Liam had done for her, despite their rocky start.

Elle and Liam gazed at one another, smiling at each other for a few extra seconds. Elle could stare into those piercing blue eyes that contrasted with brown hair all day.

Liam was treating Elle, yet again, for another meal. Elle felt almost a little guilty about all the kindness and care he had been giving her since arriving in London. She would normally attempt to reciprocate if she had more time during her day. They found their way to a quiet bench among the standing tables placed strategically near the food stands overlooking the river.

Elle looked over at Liam and laughed. "Are you trying to get sauce all over your face from the vegan hot dog?"

"Sorry, I told you that this was my favorite little food stand. The owner of the food stand is actually a chef and decided to create this little place to allow himself to spend more time in the heart of the city. I appreciate someone who takes risks to do something they believe in."

Elle noticed that Liam's face turned serious, and his comment almost took on a tone of confession.

"Have you taken some risks in your life that makes you feel so drawn to support this local treasure?"

"I have taken some risks. I moved back to England a few years ago. I was living in New York while working in the financial sector. However, my sister needed my help. I needed to be close to her, so I left everything behind to come and help her. That was three years ago, and I am now her driver for a few more years than I anticipated. It was worth it. She needed someone. Honestly, I will let her tell you that story sometime; it isn't my story to tell."

"Thank you for sharing that with me. I am sure it was hard to leave everything behind to help someone you love," Elle admitted. She wasn't sure she had anyone in her life that she would do that for, but she hoped one day she would.

"It wasn't really that hard because I was a little burnt-out by the pace of that life. I would like to do something in the future in the financial world, but I would like a little more work-life balance." Liam took another bite from his messy vegan dog.

"I completely understand that." Elle wanted to say more and tell him a bit more about her past, but she just couldn't. She opened her mouth but closed it again immediately, hoping Liam didn't notice she was holding back.

"Were you about to say something else?" Liam asked.

Just as she was trying to find the words to answer, she heard the lull of music coming from around the corner.

"Do you hear music too?"

"Do you want to join me?" Again, Liam smiled and used the *Reginald the Enchanted* line again. "I have a beautiful new kingdom to show you," Liam deadpanned, again quoting the animated feature.

"Believe it or not, I am not mad at you for your *Reginald the Enchanted* references."

Liam led Elle around the corner to a small group of people dancing to lively music. "This is called gypsy jazz music. It's fun, isn't it?"

"I love it. I feel like I have walked on the set of the movie *Choco-lat.*" Elle was looking around, taking in the sights and sounds.

People of all ages were swinging around and dancing to this music. The music had a French sound with the accordion and guitar riffs, and Elle started swaying to the music.

Liam grabbed her hand and led her to what was a makeshift dance floor. Although Elle didn't know how to swing dance, Liam led her away from him and then pulled her body back to her with the fast rhythm of the music. He swung her around under his arm and pulled her back to him with the timing of the fast-paced music. He swung her out, twirled her again, and drew her back again just as the music changed to a slower song.

Without words, Elle and Liam fell into a slow rhythm of dancing. He drew her up to him and placed her hand behind the small of her back, drawing her even closer. Elle's body warmed up immediately even though there was a chill in the air.

"Do you come here often to dance?"

"Actually, I have never danced here before. I have never had any-one I wanted to bring here before now." Liam's eyes dipped down-ward, revealing almost a shy, nervous smile.

Elle's stomach fluttered; she hadn't felt this way toward someone like this in a long time, if not ever. She had never been this excited about spending time with anyone. The two were still swaying with the music and were standing face to face. Their noses were almost touching, and they were looking at one another in anticipation. Elle drew closer to him, leaning in to him and grazing him so slowly with her nose nuzzling close to his cheek. They both stopped swaying with the music, and Liam brought up his hand to the side of her face. This time, Liam brought his face to hers and paused while staring into her eyes. He squeezed her back and pulled her even closer to him.

Elle noticed that her heart was racing as she was standing face to face with Liam. Both were standing in the middle of the makeshift dance floor, holding one another. Elle couldn't think of a more romantic moment but worried that this seemed so sudden. She wanted to kiss Liam so badly. Her hands were shaking, her stomach fluttering nervously, and she moved her face closer to his. Elle dismissed all of the doubts in her mind and brought her mouth slowly closer to his, feeling Liam's hand gently caressing the back of her neck and anticipating the gesture when Elle's phone dinged, bringing them both back to reality.

"I've got to check this since Margaux is out with Callum tonight." Elle was caught between obligation to keep Margaux safe while also attempting to have a moment that was only for her.

As she was staring at her phone, another message popped up. This time, Elle saw a message from Prina: *Dinner tomorrow tonight? I have some great news for you!* Elle replied, *Absolutely, text me details for a place you would like and within walking distance of my hotel and a time. Hugs, friend. Thank you for your help!*

"Sorry Liam, everything is ok. Do you mind if we get going? I feel like I need to get back to better prepare for tomorrow." Elle was suddenly apprehensive of this strong connection between them and her confidence she felt when she almost kissed Liam was suddenly gone. Yet, her hands were still shaken from the connection that had intensified so quickly between them. She hoped that Liam didn't feel rejected because Elle wanted to get to know him but didn't want to rush things either, even if their future, if there was one, was unclear to say the least.

"I do have one more thing to show you." Liam grabbed Elle's hand and guided her further down the cobblestone walkway.

"Mind your step here." Liam guided her over an uneven place on the sidewalk. He placed his hand underneath her arm and led her with her elbow using his other hand. "Almost there, just a few more steps. Ok, here."

Elle could see a small group of people standing together and taking photos. Liam and Elle approached the area, and she could see the space more clearly. In front of her was a Femme Frequency mural.

"Oh. My. Femme. Frequency," Elle stuttered out of her mouth. Elle grabbed Liam and gave him the biggest hug. "You are incredible. Seriously, I have been a fan forever and this is amazing. I don't know how you notice all the things that you notice about people. Will you get a picture for me?" Elle stood with a wide smile in front of the bigger-than-life Femme Frequency mural. "Come here and get a photo with me." Elle grabbed Liam and embraced him for a quick selfie. As Elle was taking the photos, Elle could see a message come across her phone from Margaux.

Elle, could you come get me now? I am kind of freaking out was on her screen.

Elle showed her screen to Liam.

"Let's go. Have her share her location and tell her we are on our way." Liam guided Elle quickly toward the car so that they could get to Margaux.

Chapter 17

"**S**he just messaged and said she is located outside a place called My Secret Stache in Essex. She said she is standing on the corner just outside of the pub." Elle stared at her phone while giving Liam the update.

"Does she always hang out in such dodgy places?" Liam asked.

"Honestly, I don't know. She loves to experience life, especially in the world of the rich and famous. Of course, I don't know if Callum Jones is famous or dodgy, but he is one of the artistic types. She seemed to be relatively calm in her texts, so hopefully there is no emergency," Elle continued.

In a short amount of time, Elle and Liam pulled up into the neighborhood of Essex and immediately saw flashing lights and bobbies were everywhere. Elle's heart fell wondering where Margaux was in the middle of the fray. She prayed that Callum and Margaux were safe.

Elle could see Margaux standing on the corner and wanted to practically leap out of the car to her. As they pulled up closer, Elle could see Margaux standing among a group of bobbies laughing.

Elle got out of the car and approaches Margaux the moment that Liam pulled up to the group.

"Are you ok?" Elle asked as she approached Margaux.

"Thank you for coming to get me. It was pretty intense for a little while, but thankfully, I had these amazing men that came to our rescue." Margaux smiled and appeared to be flirting with the group of police officers standing in a circle. "Seriously, I don't know what I would have done without them," she gushed. "Callum … Callum," Margaux called for him. "Oy!" she yelled toward him, and he turned his head.

"That was shambles," Callum laughed and hugged Margaux. "Who wants to stop for fish and chips on the way home?"

Elle was dumbfounded and realized that Callum was probably enjoying the chaos that ensued during their night out.

"Bye, Otto! See you, Uncle J!" Callum shouted over his shoulder as the group made their way from the chaos of the crowd and group of police officers. "So, do you want to go out for breakfast or something? Is that what I heard you do in the States after a night out? We will have time to go somewhere else if you want to go. Who is game for some adventure?" Callum said with enthusiasm and showing a mischievous grin.

"Margaux, what happened tonight? Also, why did you need a ride home? I am glad to help you, but it looks like you had it under control … well … a bit under control," Elle asked while trying to hide her irritation of being called like there was a dire emergency.

"We went to different pubs, and one of Callum's friends had words with some guys at a different pub and we ran into them again.

So, there was some shoving, yelling, and the next thing you know the cops arrived. One of the cops, I mean, bobbies, told me I would have to be picked up by someone, so I called you. I didn't realize until after I called that Callum is related to half of the police force in Essex, so it was all ok. I was so distracted by all of the fun that I forgot to text you back. I am so sorry." Margaux gave Elle a big hug and was leaning on Elle for support. "Did I mention that I exchanged snaps with one of the cute bobbies? He came to my rescue kind of like Liam did for you the other day." Margaux shared too much to Elle's dismay.

Elle's eyes widened after Margaux's comment about Liam rescuing her. Liam's shoulders seem to broaden with the compliment.

"Let's get some food for both of you." Elle pulled Margaux toward her. "Callum, do you want to join us for some food? I think you both need to eat something before heading home."

"No, I'll pass because we are going by my Aunt Eleanor's house. She throws down some amazing fish and chips. She will be furious if I don't come by tonight. It's a little late, but she loves my late stops when I am in Essex. Who wants to meet my aunt and get some proper fish and chips?"

Liam chimed in, "Let's go. I would love to meet your aunt, and I think both of these women should have some proper homemade fish and chips."

Elle noticed that Liam seemed to be enjoying this situation and thought he noticed how uncomfortable she was with the chaos of the scene and the unfamiliar neighborhood.

Liam leaned over Elle and whispered, "Don't worry, I would love to rescue you again if the neighborhood gets too scary," Liam dead-panned.

"You keep showing me a new kingdom," Elle countered, and Liam guffawed.

Callum was on his phone and talking to the group at the same time. His aunt was just around the corner, so Callum pointed out all of places he used to visit as a kid in this neighborhood while he waved or high-fived the occasional pedestrian despite the late hour. Elle marveled at how Callum, although a bit uncouth, could work a room, or in this case, the public street, and everyone loved to see him. "Here we are." Callum got out and opened up a gate.

The group entered the house and the smell of fresh fish and chips hit them.

"Did your aunt know we were coming?" Elle looked surprised.

"Of course, this is not my first time for a late-night stop. Plus, I told her I had some famous stylists with me so I had to impress them. Auntie!" Callum kissed his middle-aged aunt on the cheek when he found her. She grabbed him for a hug and fussed at him for looking too thin. Callum wrapped his arms around his Aunt Eleanor's ample waist. Her brown and gray hair was tied up on top and she had a cloth over one of her shoulders as though she had been using it while cooking. She looked completely thrilled to have the opportunity to feed a room full of unexpected guests. She wiped her hands on the cloth draped over her shoulder.

"Nice to meet you. Callum mentioned that you are famous stylists. It's an honor to have you here in my home. Have a seat and have something to eat. Do you like vinegar with your fish and chips?" Callum's aunt welcomed them with the offering of food.

"Honestly, I haven't ever tried them," Margaux confessed.

"Oh dahling, we are going to give you the royal treatment," Aunt Eleanor said to her, as she was loading up a plate of food for her. "We are giving you a proper welcome to Essex, bird. I am sure my sweet nephew probably introduced you to the seedier side of town tonight," she teased as she gave Callum a kiss on the cheek.

"Bollocks," Callum protested with a mouth full of food. "It was a lovely gathering of gentlemen until a bunch of punks started some trouble, and my mates ended it. It's ok because Uncle J was there so he took care of it."

Aunt Eleanor gave Callum another kiss on his cheek like he was an eleven-year-old-boy. "Do you want some more chips, love?" This time she turned her attention to Liam. Elle was trying to figure out if the middle-aged woman was flirting with Liam or just had a playful manner.

"No, thank you, ma'am. This is delicious, but I couldn't possibly eat another bite. I have to watch my waist," Liam joked and patted his stomach.

"Codswallop! You look like you were carved like a statue. Load up on some more love." Aunt Eleanor gave Liam a gentle tap on the shoulder and Liam blushed.

Elle giggled at the action because Liam literally was embarrassed by Callum's middle-aged aunt flirting with him.

"Thank you, Aunt Eleanor, but I have to get these ladies back to their hotel for the night. They have a big day tomorrow, and they need to get some rest after this amazing meal. You have outdone yourself." Liam stood up and gave Aunt Eleanor a hug before she could protest. However, she was pleased that she earned a hug from such a charming, good-looking man like Liam based on her giddiness.

"He is so adorable, Elle. He is always looking out for us. I am so glad he is really into you," Margaux said to Elle about Liam in front of everyone.

Elle was completely embarrassed by her honesty, but she gave Liam a nervous smile. Elle was surprised to see that Liam didn't see embarrassed at all by the comment, but smiled at Margaux who had enough nerve to say what he was thinking.

"Callum, do you need a ride?" Liam asked. Elle again marveled at his kind nature and his need to always take care of people.

"Thanks mate, but I am sleeping at my auntie's tonight. I'll see you in the morning though." With Callum's response, Aunt Eleanor was so pleased she had the opportunity to host an unexpected guest. Elle had the feeling that these late-night visits from Callum were not only a regular occurrence, but also something that brought his aunt great joy.

The group headed out the door and offered hugs to Callum and Aunt Eleanor. As they were leaving, Liam shouted to Eleanor, "Thank you so much!" and gave her the heart sign with his hands.

Elle smiled at his sweet interaction, which made Callum's aunt start waving her hand away with her dish towel in hand in a don't-fuss -over-me-manner.

"It seemed like you thought I was talking to you when I yelled at Aunt Eleanor," Liam joked. "You looked at me as though I was talking to you."

"Actually, Eleanor is my formal name, but I go by Elle."

"Well, you are quite the mystery Eleanor, I mean Elle." Liam's smile widened.

"You have no idea." Elle smiled back, trying to act like her comment was a joke, but secretly the feeling of shame over what was said made her stomach drop. She knew Liam had no idea all the ways and things Elle was still holding back from him.

Chapter 18

Despite the late night, Elle and Margaux made plans to arrive promptly at the fashion house in the morning, regardless of the clear indication that work started later there than in the United States.

Unlike the previous morning, Axel was waiting for the women when they arrived, sitting in a chair with his arms crossed and with an indistinguishable look on his face.

"Good morning," Elle said, while trying to interpret Axel's expression.

"Which one of you is Elle?" Axel said with no indication of emotion and in a very thick British accent.

"I am." Elle smiled, trying to reflect a bit of warmth despite feeling completely uncomfortable with this uninviting reception.

"How many times have you been the lead stylist in a fashion show?" Axel interrogated her.

"This is my fir-." Elle was unable to answer before Axel rudely interrupted her. Axel almost seemed to spit out the words at her when speaking to Elle.

Elle started explaining the process of her planning. While she was talking, her mind went elsewhere. Her mouth was moving but her mind was taken to her past. This was where Elle's time in college helped her. She knew the demands of a high-stress situation and remembered always having to prove herself. She recalled the times she was doubted, not supported, and even remembered having to remind herself of her worth and God-given talent so that she could prove to the rest of the world that she was capable. Her parents were among her worst critics at times too.

Finally, Elle's thoughts returned to her conversation with Axel and finished talking. She was out of her head and waited for Axel's retort. Elle reminded herself that she at least got a few days off and had the opportunity to spend time with Lucy and Liam for a bit even if she was about to be fired.

"Well, you have rocked my world." Finally, a small movement that appears to be the hint of a smile appeared on Axel's face between the use of the clever pun and the shock on Elle's face from the compliment. "I have never ever worked with a lead stylist that had this much vision and ambition. Not only did you bring some life into this space, but you also completely captured the essence of my vision. Typically, I have to have my people correct most of what lead stylists do. But not you." Axel again revealed a confusing expression that Elle had difficulty reading.

"I am going to leave this work in your hands. Elle, I don't trust many people. Skye, oh wait, you call her something like Lucy, right? My muse told me that you were reliable, talented, and visionary. It seems like she was right. I am going to trust you with this process. I have never, ever given a lead stylist this much freedom with my work that holds my name."

Axel started gathering his drink and his clutch that he had resting next to him.

"If you are able to train your team as successfully as you have captured this vision, then you may be the best lead stylist I have ever met."

Axel started toward the door while he turned to Callum, who had just arrived. Callum looked like he actually had slept on someone's couch.

Axel barked, "Callum, you look hideous. You need to leave and return looking like you work in a fashion house in one hour. Make it happen."

"I am sorry for my delay, but I didn't expect you to be here until later. My apologies," Callum seemed to mumble.

Elle was trying to figure out the work dynamic between the two men. Callum was usually a bit rough around the edges but usually very joyful. However, he seemed nervous around Axel. Elle was trying to figure out if Callum was nervous because he was late or if Axel was a difficult person with whom to work.

"Lucky for you, Callum. I didn't quite need you yet anyway. Elle may be the most talented lead stylist I have ever met," Axel announced to the room as though it was full of people.

Before exiting the room, Axel made a quick turn to face Elle and Margaux, whose eyes had grown wide and were giving one another silent, surprised looks based on the compliment received by the very difficult-to-understand Axel.

"Don't forget, Elle. You are the lead stylist, which means you are leading a team. You may have the vision, but let's see if you can get your team to execute the essence of my idea too. If you are able to do that, then you may be the best. But if you are not able to do it, you will not work in this industry ever again … anywhere. Good luck." He turned and walked out of the door. The sounds of his shoes could be heard going down the hall.

"Sheesh," Margaux joked, "I think we have been hired by Axella DeVil. I wouldn't be surprised if he doesn't arrive tomorrow with clothes made out of fur of Dalmatian puppies."

Elle gave Margaux a reassuring look. "He is testing us and wants to see what we are made of. I am not scared; I am used to this. I am used to proving myself," Elle said with a tone of confession and commitment. Elle changed her tone to hide the true feelings she was trying to hide from Margaux. "Plus, I have the world's most talented assistant lead stylist, so we are more than ready to rock this show!" Elle said with a high-five directed to Margaux. Margaux quickly returned an over-enthusiastic high-five, and a slapping sound filled the room.

"Bloody hell. You Americans and your strange habits. Once you are finished slapping each other's hands, give me your list of what you need to prepare for tomorrow," Callum said. "Apparently, I need to go home and rethink my attire before returning to work. I would like your list before I head out so I can pick up some things."

"Don't worry, I already have a list ready." Elle smiled at Callum and handed him the list. "I'll text you if I think of anything else."

Elle was feigning confidence, but deep down, she knew that Axel's last comment struck something. She risked everything to pursue this dream of being a stylist. She had to leave behind the world she used to know to follow her dream. And now she may be at risk of losing it if things don't go well. She was worried but she didn't want Margaux to catch on to it.

Suddenly, Elle's thoughts were interrupted by a ding. Glancing at the phone, she was suspecting a message from Liam but had forgotten about dinner plans that night with Prina.

Reservations at 7:00 tonight at Bonne Nuit under Coco Lush. I can't wait for you to meet my fiancé!

I can't wait to meet him! I'll be there. Thanks for all that you are doing for my project too.

No problem at all. I have some exciting news for your project. Plus, I am bringing a plus-one for you to meet. Remember me telling you about my fiancé's doctor friend? Well, he is joining us for dinner tonight. Squeeeee!

Chapter 19

After a very full day of work, Elle was trying to remember why she thought making plans with Prina for dinner was such a good idea while still preparing for the show. Elle remembered Prina being such a matchmaker in college, so she shouldn't be surprised she was making an effort to help her meet someone. Elle didn't want to hurt Prina's feelings by canceling dinner plans, so her plan was to politely ignore the plus-one tonight. Besides, Elle really needed to find out news about the study samples that Prina had shared with colleagues.

Elle's thoughts were vacillating between the dinner plans and her work while she was preparing for her workday. Elle was thankful that she was able to get everything ready today with the help of Margaux. For being so new to the profession, Margaux had so much instinct. She helped pair the perfect models for the looks and the hair. They both studied the list that revealed the order of the show to ensure makeup and hair could easily be adjusted with each look but without having to do something entirely different. They set up each of the stylists/model stations with the supplies that they needed and the boards near them for the looks they were accomplishing. Elle and Margaux rearranged the entire space to make the makeup, clothing, and style spaces more efficient for the models to access and go through the process of changing and making slight changes to their makeup and hair.

Elle had designed a more conservative rocker look to begin the show with many of the models starting with rocker up-dos. Their looks would gradually be taken down for each change of clothes, evolving into a more authentic rocker style. By the end of the show, all models would have their hair down with an exaggerated rocker look, leading up to the presentation of Lucy, who would be THE style icon while wearing the centerpiece outfit for the show.

Elle's thoughts returned to her getting ready for dinner with Prina as she looked at herself in the mirror of her hotel room. She just felt pangs of guilt when thinking of approaching the blind date scenario. Elle knew Prina well and this man probably looked like a Greek-god statue. She was really happy with how things were going with Liam, even if she didn't quite know how or what would happen in the future. Liam made her furious from time to time, but he was also protecting people he loved, which Elle could respect. Elle would enjoy having a fiercely protective person in her corner too.

Elle put in her earrings and decided to go for the 2-inch heels, not the 3-inch heels. She didn't want to look like she was going on a date, but she was also going to have dinner with not one, not two, but with three doctors and didn't want to look unprofessional. She decided she was going for a more professional look rather than a date look.

Elle gently knocked on Margaux's hotel room door as she was heading out for the date and asked her, "So, you are going to go out with Callum tonight, right? What did you guys end up planning?

Hopefully, the police will not need to be called tonight too."

"Actually," Margaux said in an exaggerated tone, "the police will be there tonight." Margaux smiled.

"I am confused. You are pre-planning your madness and mayhem?"

"Not exactly. Callum ran into one of his police officer relatives on his way to the fashion house this morning. Anyway, I guess a group of them are going out tonight, and I got invited. I guess there is an Irish place that has an amazing sing-along band, so I am tagging along with them."

"At least when the cops are called tonight, they will already be there with you," Elle teased.

"Funny girl," Margaux rebounded with a sarcastic look. "Have fun tonight with your college friend, right?"

"Yes ma'am. She is actually my old college roommate. We were quite close at one time when I lived an entirely different life." Elle practically whispered the last part of her sentence.

"I didn't know much about your college days; you'll have to tell me some of your wild stories some time."

"Sure thing," Elle laughed lightly, but knew that she had no intention of talking about those days to Margaux. Those days were part of a painful time in her life she put behind her.

Elle walked to the hotel entrance and checked her phone one more time for a message from Liam. He had sent her encouraging texts throughout the day so she felt a bit guilty about not seeing him tonight. Elle walked out of the entrance of the hotel and was about to order an Uber when she saw her friend's beautiful face.

"Hello, beautiful," a familiar voice cooed outside of the car in front of Elle's hotel.

"Prina!" She smiled. "I thought we were meeting at the restaurant. I am so glad you are here though," Elle corrected herself to not offend her old friend. Elle slid into the back seat of the car and sat behind her friend.

"Cliff doesn't get to drive around too much in the city, so he offered to come get you. He is quite the thoughtful guy." Prina looked lovingly over at her fiancé.

"I feel like I already know you," Cliff answered with a smile and a slightly southern American accent. "It is great to meet you. I feel like I know you already based on some of the stories that Prina shared of your college days. I am Prina's fiancé if you haven't figured that out yet," Cliff joked.

"Hello there." Elle shook Cliff's hand awkwardly over the back seat of the car.

They made small talk during the drive, and Elle could easily see how the couple fell in love. Both were doctors and doing their residency in London. Elle didn't really see Cliff as the pediatrician type, but he had such a big, charming personality. Hearing Prina and Cliff talk made Elle want to be in a relationship like that. They both were finishing each other's sentences and were both enamored with one another; it was pretty adorable.

They pulled up to the valet at the restaurant and got out. Cliff handed over his keys and Elle laid eyes on the most beautiful man she had ever seen in her life. She wasn't really looking for anyone because she wanted to see where this thing went with Liam, but Prina picked quite the looker for the date.

"Hello there, my name is Alex Moustakas." He held out his hand for Elle to shake.

Elle's mouth must have been slightly agape because based on his last name, Prina set her up with a Greek-god statue … but in human form.

Once seated at the table, the wine began to flow, and Elle found herself relaxing a bit. She not only had been nervous about being set up on a date that she wasn't interested in being on, but she was nervous how much her college years would come up as a topic of conversation. Prina knew how Elle felt about that part of her life and did a great job of avoiding the topic until Alex began asking questions about it.

"I hear you were studying dermatology too. What made you change your mind about the medical profession?" Alex asked with a true interest in Elle's answer.

Elle swallowed hard.

"She just had a change of heart," Prina interrupted. Alex could clearly see by the reply and Elle's reaction to Prina that there was more to the story.

Much to her surprise, Elle began, "I was in medical school and had an experience in the burn unit where I was volunteering for one of my required course hours. I offered to style a girl's hair who was in the burn unit because she and I had been talking during my round. She had painful burns on most of her body, but her hair was intact for the most part. I had some hair products with me from a late night the night before and asked her if I could style her hair. She was such a sassy preteen girl, and I remember how much having something like your hair styled could make you feel completely differently about yourself.

"Well, I styled her hair, and she loved it. I showed her the style in the mirror, and she cried. I cried and held her hand." A tear slowly fell down Elle's cheek, and she could feel her chin tremble. "This girl had some of the most painful burns that someone could have, but the thing that made her cry was feeling beautiful again. We cried happy tears. I wanted that for my career; I wanted happy tears and instant transformation. So, I quit medical school." Elle held her head down slightly to discreetly wipe the tear from her cheek and to allow herself a deep breath.

"I think I want to do what you do for a living. Where do I sign up?" Alex joked, and Elle was thankful for the remark so that all eyes were off of her.

Prina looked at Elle with concerned eyes from across the table. She knew there was more to the story, knew all the pain that came as a result of this choice.

"Elle is one of the smartest and most generous people I know. She is actually going to do hair in the morning in the burn unit for some teens we have there. She filled out paperwork to make sure she can come and do the volunteering. Plus, did she mention she is the lead stylist in a show for Axel Scott? Annnnnd, she was the brains behind Skye Reynolds famous rocker haircut?" Prina cooed.

Elle was officially embarrassed by all the attention and compliments.

"She is the real deal," Alex said with a long stare into Elle's green eyes. Elle could feel her stomach constrict as she could see that Alex was obviously flirting with her.

"I have to get going." Elle practically jumped out of her seat, making a noisy clang with the silverware on the table. Everyone at the table jumped. "I am sorry. I am just feeling a bit anxious about volunteering in the morning while also meeting the style team tomorrow. I have to train some people that I have never met to pull off this show, and let's just say that artsy style people can be a bit prickly," Elle said while standing. She noticed her napkin was still stuck to her lap as she was standing and tried to hide her embarrassment by calmly placing the napkin on the table and straightening the silverware she shuffled during her abrupt attempt to get up from the table.

"There's no need to rush. We can get you back to your hotel in minutes," Prina insisted.

"I can take you back to your hotel if you like. I would be happy to do it," Alex offered too.

"Oh no, thank you. Prina, I will see you in the morning at the hospital, right?" Elle made her way around the room. She shook Cliff's hand and gave Prina a hug. "I think I could get you a ticket to this. Would you like to come?" Elle asked Prina as she was hugging her goodbye.

"I would love that," Alex cooed.

Elle looked at Prina with wide eyes after Alex's comment.

"I would love to come to your debut." Prina gave Elle a long hug. "Sorry, I didn't realize he would come on so strong. Duly noted," Prina whispered.

Elle made her way to Alex and awkwardly held out her hand to give him a shake goodbye. Alex reached around her to give her a hug goodbye while simultaneously giving her a kiss partly on her mouth and partly on her cheek. Elle was dumbfounded. Did he just kiss me? In a restaurant? In front of everyone in this space? A guy that just met me an hour ago?

"Goodbye." Elle quickly grabbed her purse and turned to make her way out of the restaurant when she noticed two very familiar eyes looking back at her near the exit of the restaurant. Elle's stomach tightened when she saw Liam staring at her with a shocked and hurt look on his face.

Chapter 20

"Hey there, what are you doing here?" Elle asked Liam when she walked outside of the restaurant, almost shocked by seeing him and trying to act casual, unsure if he just witnessed the kiss debacle.

"I just came to pick up some takeaway. It looks like you have your hands full." Liam had a combined look of irritation or disdain. He glanced over Elle's shoulder at Alex, who was waving in their direction.

Then, Elle started speaking so quickly as though her words couldn't come out fast enough to explain why he would have seen her kissing a random guy in a restaurant. "I met my college friend and her fiancé for dinner. She invited a guy, and I had no idea that I was being set-up, and anyway he was coming on a little strong and…" Elle was trying to explain why he would have seen Alex kissing her much to her dismay. She felt terrible and couldn't believe the Greek god, Alex, had been coming on so strong.

As she was trying to explain herself in the fastest way possible, she could see Liam's posture become more rigid after she said Alex had been coming on strong.

"You don't need to explain yourself to me," Liam continued as though he and Elle hadn't had the most romantic moment of her entire life last night.

Elle stepped closer to him and lowered her voice to a whisper. "Honestly, I had no idea he was going to be here until this afternoon, let alone kiss me goodbye. It was so weird and awkward for him to do that. Prina invited him, and I didn't want to cancel the chance to see my dear friend. By the way, I am excited about whatever we have going on between us, and I am not the kind of girl to go exploring other options while I am getting to know you. I am being completely honest and wouldn't want to jeopardize what we have between us, even if it is new." Elle could see Liam's posture tense up even more when she was speaking to him. Liam, the protector, was beginning to emerge from his shell.

Given his history of being an overprotective brother with Lucy, she thought she made a big mistake, letting him know that Alex was coming on too strong. Liam's posture was rigid, and his mouth had become a straight line. She saw his jaw clench and wondered why Liam's reaction was so firm when she felt a hand slide up her lower back from behind her. Now, Elle's posture had become rigid.

Alex approached Elle and Liam as they were talking. "Hey there, I am Alex. I am Elle's date." Alex held his hand out for Liam while his other hand remained on the lower part of Elle's back.

Elle's posture remained stiff, and she tried her best to show that his advances were not welcome without making it awkward in front of her friend. She was absolutely shocked that Alex was coming on so strong and would touch her lower back in such an intimate way. She was also baffled by Alex's behavior as Prina set her up with a guy like him. Despite just meeting her an hour ago, it was like Alex was trying to stake some claim on Elle after he saw Liam with her. Elle was far from impressed by the behavior and knew too many men who acted just like him; this was a pride maneuver and not the actions of a gentleman, Elle thought. She stepped away from Alex's unwanted affection.

Liam ignored Alex's outstretched hand. "Funny, Elle was just telling me she didn't even know you were coming for dinner. That seems like a weird date. You may want to ask your date if she actually wants to be kissed before you make a move on her. I mean are you still in primary school to make a move like that on a woman?" Liam's tone was inexpressive and serious.

"Are you her dad or something?" Alex joked and moved his hand to touch Elle's back again, but she had already stepped away from reaching distance.

Liam stepped even closer to Alex and brought his voice down to a whisper. "I am her hired driver for the week. I am in charge of her well-being. One part of my job is to protect her from a dishy bloke like yourself." Liam smiled through gritted teeth. "You need to confirm this with Elle yourself, but based on what I am seeing, she is not interested."

"Am I bothering you, Elle?" Alex was convinced his charm would work on Elle without question. "I thought we were having a great time. Am I bothering you, Elle?" Alex's slimy smile widened over his overconfident face.

"Actually, I have to get going, Alex. Have a great evening." Elle held out her hand to shake Alex's hand.

"Give me a call," Alex said, almost taunting Liam.

"Do you want this bloke to call you, Elle?" Liam asked her, making an effort to be clear about her intentions.

"I'll pass on the call, but have a great evening," Elle replied. Elle was trying her best to be civil; after all, this was an acquaintance of one of her dearest friends, but she was completely not interested in him in the least.

"Did you hear that, Alex? She won't be calling, and she doesn't want you to call. Got it? You are done as far as Elle is concerned. Do you understand that, Alex?" Liam said. Liam appeared to be pouring salt in Alex's wounds, but instead, he was making it crystal clear that his advances ended there. Elle had seen this protective version of Liam before and was impressed with his calm, but confident demeanor.

"Got it." The look on Alex's face made it clear that he had no understanding how his charm was not working on Elle or Liam.

Prina and Cliff then walked up to the now growing group of people. "I didn't know you were still here," Prina gushed while approaching the group. Elle was thankful for the interruption because Prina's bubbly personality could crack even this awkward moment.

"Hello, I am Liam." He held out his hand to Prina and Cliff. His stress seemed to fall away from him, and it was the old charming man who Elle became so interested in getting to know. As usual, Liam dismissed his significant role in Elle's life, but it was enough to keep the conversation light and allow everyone to part ways. Before walking out the door, Prina called out, "Elle, don't forget to see me as soon as you arrive at the hospital tomorrow because I have some news on your little project." Prina's smile widened.

Elle's stomach churned because Liam didn't know about Elle's project, and Elle's mind began to race about what the news may be. Regardless, if it was terrible, Prina wouldn't have mentioned it like she did. Elle was confident she didn't need to worry about it and would get some details tomorrow.

"I am sorry you got involved with that," Elle said to Liam as they were leaving the restaurant. "Don't you need to grab your food before we leave?" Elle asked Liam.

"It's not important anymore. I just want to make sure you get where you need to go next safely. I can't stand a guy like that," Liam mentioned. "I grew up with money, but I have never been an entitled jerk … ever. Where can I drive you next?" Liam's tone seemed to change immediately after leaving the restaurant.

"Liam." Elle turned to face him. "I didn't know about the date. Prina mentioned setting me up, but I thought she meant that sometimes she would do it, like a joke. I didn't think it was going to happen now or ever. I didn't realize she would actually do it while I was here this week. I just want you to know that I am not hiding that from you." She took Liam's hand. "Besides, I want to see where this thing goes with us." She took Liam's hand and intertwined her fingers through his.

"Look, we are both busy with work, and I know we are juggling so much right now. I don't need to explore this if it isn't going anywhere. I need to be able to trust you," Liam whispered to Elle.

"I am sorry if I broke your trust. I really do like you." Elle looked up over shy eyes.

"That's good because I really like you too." Liam stepped closer to Elle. He brushed her hair past her shoulder and placed his hand on her cheek, brushed her cheek with his thumb.

"I liked to ask, unlike Alex, if I can kiss you one day," Liam confessed, making Elle's stomach flip.

Elle loved that he didn't attempt to kiss her right here and now, but just left it as a promise that one day it would happen at the right time. Again, Elle felt that Liam was unlike any other man she had ever known.

"While we are being honest, I do have one more thing that I want you to know."

Liam stopped moving toward Elle and steadied himself, waiting to see what secret she was about to share.

Chapter 21

"Let's go to the car. I need to have some privacy while I share what I am going to tell you." Elle led Liam toward the car. "Oh wait, where is the car? I forgot I didn't come with you here." Elle and Liam both looked at each other and laughed, but Liam seemed a bit subdued because Elle noticed the laughter didn't quite make it to his eyes.

Elle continued to lead him to the car until she found it. After getting in the car, Elle could see that Liam's mind seemed consumed or distracted. She could assume it was because he was wondering where this conversation was going.

"Ok, I am going to tell you about one of the most difficult parts of my life, but it relates to what is going on tonight. Just bear with me because I don't like to really speak about it, but I know it is still impacting me regardless of how much I try to pretend it doesn't. Ok." Elle took a deep breath, and she could feel the throaty sensation when you are trying to fight back tears.

"Ok, here it goes," Elle repeated again and took an even longer breath. "Prina and I were in medical school together. We were both studying to be dermatologists. I loved the idea of making a difference in the lives of others. For one reason or another, I tended to gravitate toward working with those in the burn unit during my studies. Well into medical school, I had to get some hours at a hospital, and I signed up to go to a burn unit to get some hours and to help serve. The purpose of the class I was in was to gain experience actually seeing the reality of the areas of the hospital without being too hands-on at this point. The program I was in really invested time in helping us find our niche in the medical community before getting too far into our program with our specialty area that may not suit us in the long run."

"How long ago was this?" Liam asked attentively and touched Elle's hand in reassurance as he sat next to her behind the wheel and she sat looking into his eyes while in the passenger seat.

"Just about five years ago," Elle said with a small smile.

"I volunteered in a unit with mostly kids one day. I met a girl named Isabella. She had some of the most painful burns one could have. Strangely enough, her hair was fully in-tact and not impacted by her burns. She and I talked about celebrities and style. I asked her if I could style her hair; ironically, I had some of my hair products with me because I had a late night the night before. So, I styled her hair. This beautiful girl had some of the most painful burns on her body and was nothing but pure joy. Once I revealed her styled hair to her, she cried happy tears because she felt beautiful again. She cried, and I cried too. I decided after that day that I wanted something like that for the rest of my life with my work." Elle's chin started to tremble.

Liam took her hand into his and brought her hand up to his mouth, kissing the back of her hand. He didn't really understand how this was so painful, but he was ready to learn more about Elle.

Liam encouraged Elle. "I can't imagine making that kind of decision. You are so brave to know exactly what you wanted and to stop what you were doing and change your life entirely."

Liam's reassuring words just poured over her.

Elle took a deep breath to fight her quivering chin and the strange sensation invading her throat as she continued to fight back tears.

"My decision wasn't the hardest part for me; what came next was. I knew my parents expected me to stay in this field. I grew up being raised from the mindset that only certain career paths were worthy. Plus, I had always been one of the brightest students in my school in the area of math and science. I took Biology I in middle school.

"I knew telling my parents would be the hardest part because I didn't know how they would take the decision I had made. I knew that they always enjoyed seeing me pursue the dream of becoming a doctor. Aside from church, this was the second most important thing in their lives, helping me pursue this dream. I never once questioned if they would still love me for who I wanted to be if I wasn't a doctor." A tear escaped Elle's corner of her eye, and she quickly wiped it away.

"Lucy and I came from a very non-traditional family. I can understand the strange complexities of family expectations more than you may know," Liam said and gently rubbed Elle's neck and shoulder as they sat side by side in the car.

"I don't talk about this to anyone … ever. After I told my parents about my decision, they disowned me. I was told that I had to repay back the money they spent on my education. My biggest fear with making this decision came true. My parents' love was conditional … on the condition that I did exactly what they wanted me to do," Elle said in almost a whisper, and tears were poised at the edge of Elle's eyes. "I don't even care about paying them back the money; it is just that I don't see my parents as the loving and kind people that I thought they were my entire life."

"I am baffled that your parents find being a stylist so terrible. I mean, why is nothing else good enough? You are still helping people, right?" Liam looked at Elle, trying to better understand while offering some comfort to her. He did know, after working for Lucy, how shallow the industry can be, but Elle wasn't like anyone he had met in that field. Didn't her parents see that about her?

"I grew up in the church and as I look back, I think my parents felt that only some jobs are worthy for a Christian to have. If not, I was not walking in faith in their eyes. I can still go to church, go on mission trips, and have a strong walk with my faith, but not having the 'right' career path in their eyes is morally wrong." Elle stopped so that she would not get too emotional. "I have always seen my parents as such upstanding, loving people, but this has changed the way I see them. I don't like feeling this way about them either, despite the hurt I feel.

"I don't regret my decision, but I am still heartbroken about finding out who my family really is with their faith. I thought they were the pillars of my old community and of my old church family. They aren't who I thought they were, and that is equally as difficult as the rejection. I am still a Christian, but it hurts that they think I am not because of my work. Honestly though, I would love to have them back in my life, even if the relationship isn't quite the same. I miss them." Elle shrugged her shoulders as though she couldn't believe that she hoped to make amends after some time had passed.

Elle took a minute to stare out the window, looking away from Liam. He didn't interrupt her but just gently rubbed her hand in reassurance.

"So, the night I met your sister, I was able to pay myself for the first time since I moved into my new shop when she left the 'tip' she gave me. Up until then, I have been living off my savings, and all my earnings go to Margaux or paying back my parents. After this fashion show is over, I will have my parents completely repaid from medical school. I won't owe them anything anymore. Your sister's offer for me to help with this show is life-changing for me. I won't be carrying the guilt of owing them the money anymore."

"Did you try to talk to your parents after you left medical school?"

"I did, but they won't have anything to do with me. They wouldn't let me come home to regroup or come up with my Plan B. I have been on my own since I decided to leave medical school."

"So, did you come see Prina to reconnect with an old friend?"

"Actually, I am working on a little project with Prina. Remember how I told you I am really good at math and science? Well, I would like for you to come to the hospital with me tomorrow before I go to the fashion house so you can hear about my little project. I wanted to talk to Prina about it tonight, but Dr. McHandsy cut my evening short," Elle attempted a joke. "Would you like to come with me to the hospital tomorrow?"

"Elle, I don't think I can possibly say no to you. It would be my honor to accompany you tomorrow at the hospital." With that,

Liam wiped a tear away from the corner of Elle's eye, gently placing the palm of his hand against her face and gazing into her eyes, not to make a move but to show that he truly appreciated her sharing this with him. It was such an intimate and loving gesture that Elle's heart felt such an overwhelming feeling of gratitude and it began pounding in her chest.

"You are one of the most beautiful, brave, and incredible people I have ever met. Thank you for sharing your story with me. I appreciate your honesty, but I know it must have been hard to talk about it."

With a wry, little grin, he said, "I have to say, Elle Bennett, you are full of surprises." Liam then smiled.

"If you think I am full of surprises now, wait until tomorrow," Elle said and she returned the wry grin.

Chapter 22

A s usual, Liam arrived on time with a Coco Lush oat milk latte in hand the next morning.

"Good morning, beautiful." Liam handed over the coffee to Elle as she opened the passenger door. "I was going to come around and get the door for you, but you are too fast. How do you look so amazing after only a few hours of sleep last night?" Liam was grinning from ear to ear.

"Let me grab all your supplies and put them in the back. Do you need anything else?" Liam called, while standing behind the car so that Elle couldn't see him.

"Well, I don't know about looking beautiful, but I am so ready for this. Are you ready to go to the hospital?" Liam seemed to be eagerly anticipating the visit to the hospital and potentially more news about Elle's project.

"Let's do this. I am ready to volunteer and hear some news about my project. I pray that everything will go well with my new team too for the fashion show. I try to plan for everything while also trying to expect the unexpected."

Liam gave her hand an encouraging squeeze.

Once they entered the hospital, they were greeted by Prina, who also had some carts ready for Elle to bring up her styling supplies.

Prina was her usual ray-of-sunshine self. "Good morning! I hope you don't mind that I brought a cart for you to take your supplies upstairs," Prina said in a sing-song tone while giving Elle a big hug and simultaneously holding her hand out for Liam to shake in the strangest way. Liam and Prina laughed at her effort.

"Let's go upstairs. I will give you the update about your project later if you can wait a bit longer," Prina said with a bit of a nervous smile.

"I have been waiting for this idea to come together for years, so I am sure I can wait a few more hours," Elle teased.

Elle felt a flutter in her stomach as they approached the children's wing of the burn unit. She felt so honored by being able to serve here; if it wasn't for Prina, she would have never been given the ok to come and work with the kids that day. She loved doing that.

Prina brought her to her first room where Elle met Jayna. Prina and Jayna clearly were familiar with one another because Prina and Jayna didn't just say hello but broke into an impromptu handshake-almost-dance that looked rehearsed.

"Impressive! I don't have those kinds of skills, Jayna," Elle admitted.

"Oh no, Jayna, she doesn't; Elle is one of my oldest friends," Prina said.

"What? Do you actually have a friend?" Jayna teased Prina so quickly that Elle could see why the two of them seemed so close.

"Gotcha!" Elle cackled.

"It is true. I have only one friend, but Miss Elle here has some famous friends. Do you want to know whose hair she styled recently? She gave Skye Reynolds's her new haircut. Can you even believe it?" Prina said, almost embarrassing Elle.

Elle knew some kids take their time getting to know people here at the hospital, and she was sure Prina was using this to help Jayna get to know Elle better.

"Are you serious? What are you doing here? Shouldn't you be counting your millions and jet-setting with the rich and famous?" Jayna teased.

"I usually just count my millions on Tuesday, so that would make me free this morning," Elle countered with a smile.

Liam was standing near the door of the room, staying rather quiet but admiring Prina and Elle on their ability to connect with this girl. Liam guessed she was around fourteen years old and knew how hard it too could be to connect with someone that age, yet they made it look effortless.

"Who is the creepy guy standing by the door looking, sus?" Jayna asked.

Elle was impressed that she didn't miss a thing.

"He is my driver for the week while I am here. I usually live in NYC," Elle shared.

"Oy! Come over here a bit. I don't bite hard." Jayna loved making Liam uncomfortable as he was doing his best to remain unnoticed.

"So, tell me, Elle, how does one come to London for the week, get a Bev driver at your fingertips, and have the pleasure of hanging with me?" Jayna was on a roll.

With Jayna's sassy attitude, Elle would have never thought this girl was injured let alone burned, alongside a good part of her body. Elle marveled at this girl's bravery and grit.

"Well, I will tell you the story of how I came to be in London if you trust me to do your style this morning. If Skye Reynolds can trust me, do you trust me to give you a style this morning? Prina said you are an icon, and I need to give you a style to match your moxie. Do you like Skye's look or do you like a classic style?" Elle began.

Liam watched in awe. He watched how Elle built such an easy connection with this girl so quickly. Jayna asked about her favorite movies but admitted that the book was always better than the movie. They talked about London and how Jayna always wanted to visit NYC. Of course, Elle offered her a free style for her visit when she made it there. Elle was mindful of her burns while also making it seem like the scars were also non-existent. He marveled at the way conversation came so easily for her and could feel something in his heart soften. He admired Elle. He respected and thought that maybe he was caring more deeply for her now than ever. People in his world were not this genuine, and Elle was absolutely the most authentic person he had ever met.

"Oy! Earth to Liam!" Jayna called.

Liam snapped back to reality.

"Sorry, I was in my own head. What's up?" Liam was trying to sound like a natural responding to Jayna.

"I asked how you became a driver for Skye Reynolds. You seem a little nervous around people, so I guess someone took pity on you." Jayna loved making Liam squirm.

"You aren't wrong," Liam continued. "Skye is my sister. Let me let you in on a little secret. Her real name is Lucy, and she eats all of the yellow M&Ms out of the bag first. I mean, what kind of neanderthal does that with a perfectly good bag of M&Ms?" Liam seemed to be getting more comfortable.

"She is a savage! I can't bear to see her next movie knowing that she behaves so savagely!" Jayna joked.

"Don't even get me started on the noise she makes when she chews!" Liam continued.

"Don't continue please. I can't hear anymore!" Jayna continued pretending to be pained to hear such truth about one of her favorite celebrities.

Elle was enjoying hearing the banter between Liam and Jayna as she was finishing up the style.

"Ok, girlfriend, I think we are finished unless you have some adjustments you want me to make," Elle said as she handed Jayna a mirror. "Is there anything I can change?" Elle watched Jayna look at herself in the mirror.

The happy-go-lucky Jayna became serious, and quick tears began welling up in her eye. Elle lowered her voice to a whisper and acknowledged Jayna's burns for the first time. "I use some special products that are not only sensitive to delicate skin but guarantees to avoid any irritation; it protects it, believe it or not. I would love to do some makeup, but that isn't my specialty. What do you think about getting some of my makeup team over here one day?" Elle asked in an effort to help bring Jayna back to her jovial self.

"Are you kidding me? That would be amazing," Jayna said with a smile.

"Well, I can't make any promises, but I am meeting my makeup team today. I haven't met them, but I have a feeling they may be willing to take some time to come see you."

"I'm kind of nervous about his big week. I have so many people to lead through this show, so I would appreciate some kind thoughts for our team, ok? Do you believe in the power of prayer?" Elle asked Jayna in a somewhat vulnerable tone.

"Are you kidding? Jesus is my homie," Jayna answered quickly.

"Well, I am leading a team of stylists, makeup artists, and a design team. I am meeting many of them for the first time today. Please pray that I am a good leader and inspire everyone to work well together during the show. Do you mind praying for me? Want me to pray for you?" Elle asked.

Just like that, Liam watched Jayna and Elle join hands and pray for each other in the sweetest prayer he had ever heard. He wanted to go hug the world because Elle was showing him a world that he didn't know existed.

"Sadly, I have to get going, but you, my girl, are a treasure," Elle said to Jayna.

"I am pretty fabulous, but I try to balance it with being sarcastic, so there is that," Jayna deadpanned again.

Prina arrived and told Elle it was time to go to another girl who was waiting for her arrival.

Elle and Jayna exchanged socials quickly, and they were on to the next girl waiting for her mini-makeover.

Elle entered the next door, and Prina introduced her to Claire.

Again, Liam stood at the door watching Elle go to work with Claire so effortlessly. Despite it being such a short amount of time, Liam felt right then that he may be falling for Elle.

Chapter 23

"Elle, that was amazing, but first, Prina made me promise to bring you to her before we left the hospital. She said it had something to do with your little project. I have to admit that I have never met someone like you before … I mean … how do you find the time to do all the things that you do? What kind of project are you doing?" Liam asked, hoping to learn more about the woman that he found absolutely captivating. He had never felt like that before.

"There is my talented bestie!" Prina cooed down the hall as she tried to capture Elle's attention.

"Thank you so much for coordinating all of this. Did you find out about bringing back my makeup team later today? Did you see the products that we can use for makeup to prevent any possible irritation?" Elle asked, already coming up with a Plan B and C.

"Yes, my dear, your team has been approved to come back and do some light makeup with the teens later today. Aren't you supposed to be training your people though? Aren't you doing a little thing called a fashion show in just a few short days? I mean, I appreciate how you have always embraced the hands-and-feet-of-Jesus mentality, but I don't want you to stretch yourself too thin," Prina said, touching Elle's arm.

"If there is anything I know about people in this industry, they can be a bit bossy and self-serving. I think we may have some nastiness among the team at first while everyone is trying to make a name for themselves and stake claim on their contribution to the team. If I get any wind of it, we are coming here. There is nothing better to remind yourself that life is not about you when helping someone else in need," Elle said triumphantly. "I can guarantee we will be coming here because I think they will need the reminder that life isn't always about ourselves." Elle smiled conspiratorially.

"I love you so much," Prina said with a smile. "You have the best heart and mind. Speaking of your amazing mind, I have some good news about your trials. I can't believe you are actually here to get this information face to face. When you sent me the samples nearly a year ago, who would have thought that we would be seeing each other to review the results of it? I digress. The trials are promising. Not only are your products acting as a protectant for sensitive skin, but they also have a calming quality too. So far, all the participants have had a positive result after using your product with the exception of one person. The one person realized that they had something for lunch that was an allergen for them, so it was not your product most likely, but it was noted in the study. You did say that you applied in the States for a patent, right?" Prina asked.

"Yes, I have a patent pending. I wanted to make sure I went through the trials with the medical community too. We were able to have enough samples tested in order for me to take the next steps to making this product a reality, right?" Elle asked hesitantly, trying not to appear too hopeful.

"Elle, it looks like everything is checking out for you, my dear. This product may change everything for people that I see every day. This product can be used in so many ways. I am absolutely thrilled to see what may happen next with it. Your biggest decision is to decide what you are going to call this miracle product." Prina nearly sang the last part while finally revealing her utter excitement for her dear friend.

"I am sorry if I sound daft, but what is this product you guys are talking about? Elle, did you make some special product?" Liam asked, looking confused and feeling that Elle was again hiding something from him.

"Remember when I said I used to be in medical school? Well, when I became a hair stylist, I realized how much understanding and mixing chemicals really aren't that different from medical school in some regard. You have to know how to mix chemicals and how things will best react in hair too. I started experimenting with different compositions of chemicals after I had a highly sensitive client come for a hair appointment. Over time, I perfected my product and here I am." Elle smiled shyly, trying to avoid the attention on her at the moment and completely oversimplifying the process that took her years to perfect.

"Oh. My. Gosh. Girl. Stop. It," Prina emphasized every word. "She is being so humble. This product she designed could be a game-changer for the industry. It isn't just protecting sensitive skin, but also calming it. Using this product in makeup, hair color, or even on sensitive skin in a hospital that doesn't react well to an adhesive could use it for example. This could be used anywhere and not just in the beauty industry. My girl is being so humble because she isn't in it for the money; she wants to help people. I just love you, precious friend. I get credit for being some kind of superhero by just being in medical school, but here you are changing the world like this, and it could help people you can't even imagine." Prina said the last part with just a little quiver in her voice.

She was looking at her dear friend who received such rejection from the people she loved most, who didn't take time to understand her motivations in making a career change; yet she is doing more than Prina ever could. Prina wasn't feeling jealous but absolute joy for her friend.

"Prina, please … you know how embarrassed I get over this kind of thing," Elle pleaded.

"I know, I know … what did you use to say in college? Be the hands and feet, right? Well, my girl, you are doing it, and I couldn't be prouder to call you, my friend. The team of doctors who participated in the study want to get permission from you with some of the details of the study, but seriously, it all looks so promising. ¨

"I can't thank you enough, but I have to get going to meet my team. I'll text you later to see if we are coming back to do some makeup, but if I had to guess, I would say we are probably coming back soon." Elle smiled as though she felt confident about her plans with her new team.

"It won't be a problem at all. If I am one when you arrive, just text me, and I can come back to the hospital. Also, my amazing fiancé Cliff is available to be your guide too."

Elle hugged Prina goodbye and set out to go to the fashion house.

"I'm sorry if you have quite a few questions at this point, but I have to warn you. I wasn't hiding anything from you to keep a secret, but I didn't mention this little project of mine because I didn't want to feel disappointed if the trials didn't turn out well. I just can't believe it looks like I will have the medical assurance that this product works and is safe." Elle's voice almost fell to a whisper when she thought about this big dream actually coming true.

"You continue to amaze me, Elle. So, just to make sure I am following this. You used to be in medical school and used some of that knowledge to develop a product as a stylist that will help people with sensitive skin? Were you thinking of using this in the fashion industry? I know Prina made it sound like this could be used in a variety of settings. Was that your plan?" Liam asked, expressing genuine interest.

"Well, I have a client who has sensitive skin. Actually, she has some burns on her scalp from an accident. The scarring is sensitive to any product, and it prevents this young, vibrant girl from trying any of the things that she would like. I wanted to make sure that she could have access to anything she wanted, so I started experimenting." Elle smiled shyly.

"You make experimenting sound so easy," Liam teased.

"Well, I am very stubborn, and I take meticulous notes, thanks to medical school. I was determined to find something that would work for her. So, here we are now."

"Here we are now," Liam's smile widened, and he stepped closer to Elle. He tucked a piece of hair behind her ear. "If we weren't standing outside of a hospital, I would be tempted to kiss you right now, with your permission of course. You have no idea how hard it is for me not to take you into my arms because I feel like the luckiest man alive that someone like you would even consider spending time with a celebrity driver." Elle's pulse quickened just feeling his warm breath whisper in her ear while he was standing so close.

"You are more than just a celebrity driver. You are a protective brother who sacrificed some of his own passions in life to help protect a sister who needed him. I am lucky to be spending time with you." Elle took Liam's hand in hers, and Liam took her hand up to his mouth and gently kissed the back of her hand while staring directly in her eyes. Elle's body felt like it was on fire.

A loud horn sounded just steps from Elle and Liam, causing both of them to jump.

"Oy! Love birds, get moving! I have to pull up here to drop off a patient! Keep moving!"

"I would be tempted to yell back at the driver, but I understand what he means. So, what is this miracle product going to be called?" Liam asked as they started walking.

"Can I tell you later? It is a bit of a long story." Elle smiled sheepishly.

"For you, Elle, I'll wait for you as long as you need me to wait."

Elle's stomach fluttered because Liam's eyes suggested that he may be speaking about more than just learning the name of her new product, and Elle couldn't have been happier than this moment.

Chapter 24

Elle and Liam arrived at the fashion house and could hear bickering the moment they arrived. Elle knew that the fickle makeup team would give her a run for her money, but she tried to have everything planned to prevent any drama.

As calmly as possible, Elle entered the room where the sounds of snide remarks fell like confetti. "Hello team, I see you made yourselves at home. By home, I mean you are bickering like back-biting children. I heard that you are among the best in the industry, yet you are behaving like … like … novices … not like the icons I promised I have on my team. Alyssa, did you move your station from where I placed each of you?"

Alyssa replied, "I wanted to be closer to the window because my cell reception is terrible and I…"

"You can leave, Alyssa," Elle said in a tone that was as cold as ice.

Margaux was watching this all unfold. She couldn't believe her eyes or her ears because she had never seen Elle behave like this before. Elle was nothing but encouraging to her; however, she did see that the makeup artists were petty and competitive the moment they arrived at the fashion house. Each seemed to be proving their dominance among the other artists, and it looks like Elle was prepared for it, Margaux was thinking to herself.

"I was just…" Alyssa attempted to persuade Elle to reconsider.

"Liam, would you please escort Alyssa out of the fashion house? Be sure to take your things with you," Elle said with a stern expression.

"Thank you, Liam. Team, thank you for being here in a timely manner. I appreciate your timeliness and professionalism. My name is Elle Bennett, and I am the lead stylist for our show. We are going to go over some basics of how we are going to function for this event. I am also going to share a little about the inspiration behind the show so that you can better understand the vision. Axel Scott has entrusted us to help his vision come to fruition; as a team, only together can we do it. This isn't a competition, but we are a team.

"Additionally, this is not only reflecting on Axel Scott, but also on Skye Reynolds, who has inspired this fashion event. Unlike most shows, we would have more time to work together and more time to hone our looks. I have been placed in charge of this task, and you are the team I need to make it happen.

"Due to our tight timelines, we won't have much time to revisit different looks or to negotiate creative ideas. We need to refine our work and the looks that I have created for you on the various boards around the room. Normally, I would encourage you to put your creative mark on your work, but in this case, I need to trust that you will create this vision that has been approved by Axel Scott. If you feel like you cannot work as a team, or if you need to individualize this work, then please leave like I have just asked Alyssa to do. If you want to have an opportunity to change your professional life and make a family who loves the same work you do, then you have come to the right place. Let's get to work," Elle said confidently and firmly, like she had been rehearsing this speech.

After Elle brought the team up to speed on the work and the inspiration, she had artists examine the looks and stand in front of the board with the design that spoke to them the most. Elle had the team begin practicing the looks on another artist. She had some other tricks up her sleeve to have the artists connect a bit more as they were learning and practicing the looks for the event. Elle felt a little flutter in her stomach when she heard some laughter while some of the artists were working together. Once she saw that everyone was engaged in practicing their work, Elle called Liam over.

"Do you mind texting Prina, confirming our visit to the hospital in about an hour? Also, could you reach out to your sister to see if she could come by today? I think it will help my team connect just a bit more and find their purpose if she can come for a quick visit. I need them to know they aren't competing with each other for this show. By the way, thank you so much for all your help!"

"Team, I am now going to have you practice your looks again, but this time I want to time you doing it. You will have roughly a five-to-seven-minute window to get the makeup removed and the new look applied. I have already paired you up with a different member of the team. You are going to be judged on the time, but also the quality of the look. Callum, Axel Scott's assistant, will determine the 'quality' of your work. Let's get started."

Much to Elle's surprise, teams were working together, joking a bit, and improving their work. Callum brought on a fierce and intimidating role as judge and jury. The artists seemed to be receptive to Elle's feedback after Callum ranked the quality of the work. The room was electric with excitement while the artists were being put through the ringer in timing their work for the show.

"Ok team, you are doing amazing work, and I love to see you improving your time and quality. I am so pleased with our progress. We are taking a quick 'field trip' for a couple of hours. I have a list here of the supplies you will need to bring with you on our outing. When we return, I am going to have us work on perfecting our looks and time to complete it. Does anyone have any questions?" Elle asked.

"Where are we going?" A very unsure artist asked while raising their hand, as though they were in elementary school.

"We are going to go practice our looks on some of the toughest critics in town, but I think you are ready." Elle offered a conspiratorial smile to Margaux and Liam.

"If you say we're ready, you must see something we don't," another artist joked.

"I absolutely think you are ready for these critics," Elle offered a reassuring word.

As the artists were packing up their supplies, Elle leaned over to Liam and whispered, "Did you pay Alyssa for helping me for a couple of hours? Was she ok after I had her leave so dramatically? She understood it was also part of my plan to convince my team that I was not going to let them run over me as their lead stylist, right?"

"Of course, she understood what she was asked to do to make a quick $200 for two hours of acting work. My sister knows many struggling actors who are eager to make some easy money and to add to their resume. I'll admit that you had me convinced that you were absolutely furious," Liam whispered back to Elle.

"Do you think it worked with my team? They seem to be connecting and seeing their purpose for their work, right?" Elle asked almost just for reassurance.

"You couldn't have planned it any better. You couldn't have done any of it any better than you already have. You … are perfect." Liam held her gaze with his last comment, and Elle knew that it was going to be really hard to leave him when she went back to New York the next week.

Chapter 25

The team arrived at the hospital looking absolutely confused as to why they were there.

"Hello, my name is Dr. Prina Patel, and I am going to be guiding you today. I hear you are doing some makeup on some of our most influential people here at the hospital."

"That is what we were told," one of the artists responded to Prina.

"I am going to have Elle provide you with the details of your visit, and I will see you upstairs." Prina nodded as she made her exit.

"Team, you are going to the burn unit to do some light makeup and style for the teen's wing. I was here earlier today doing some hair with some of the patients. Prina will be leading us around to patients who are willing to do makeup with you. I also had stickers and temporary tattoos made that have the logo for the show for patients who don't want too much makeup so we can give them a little special treatment. Please stay positive. Be encouraging. I put you in teams again so that you can take turns doing makeup while the other may just have some small talk with the patients.

"These kids have endured some of the most painful and diffi-cult injuries one can endure, and yet they will love spending time with you. Each of you have supplies that are hypoallergenic and well-suited for the sensitive skin that the teens have. Does anyone have any questions?"

"Why are we doing this?" a nervous artist asked.

"Do you mind asking the same question after we are finished with our time here?" Elle stated with a smile, hiding the frustration she was feeling by someone having the audacity to not see the bigger picture. She reassured herself that it was again the reason why they need to be there.

Elle gave the partners time to get into different rooms and to be-gin doing the teens' make-up. She decided to go see Jayna when she heard laughter rolling out of the room.

"Jayna, are you entertaining my team?" Elle entered her room.

"I thought I would provide some comic relief because you are going to be working really hard over the next few days. They are going to need some laughs first," Jayna joked.

"You aren't wrong," Elle continued. "Don't let this go to your head, but the color combination with your eyes looks even better than Skye. You may have your own fashion line inspired by you soon." Elle's eyes crinkled as she smiled at Jayna.

"Whoa, whoa, whoa, let's not steal my show just yet." Elle's eyes widened as she heard a familiar voice behind her. Elle didn't turn and look but instead looked wide-eyed at Jayna, who also had a shocked expression on her face.

"Please don't tell me that Skye Reynolds just heard me tell you that you are rocking her look. That couldn't possibly have just happened, right?" Elle's mouth started to reveal a sheepish smile.

"Nah Elle, she heard it all. I think you better go look for another job," Jayna deadpanned.

"I can't fire her; she is the best in the business." Skye smiled.

"Elle is the best in the business. Wow, business must not be looking too good if she is the best. Ohhhhh!" Jayna raised her hands up as she roasted Elle properly and emphasized the joke. Jayna attempted to high-five one of the makeup artists who completely avoided the bait.

"Sorry, Elle, you walked right into that one. I couldn't help myself. Are you going to introduce me to Skye Reynolds or what?" Jayna smiled.

"So, you must be the famous Jayna that I heard so much about." Skye held out her hand.

"I tend to have that effect on people. I could tell that Elle was wowed by me," Jayna continued.

"Oh no, it was my brother Liam who told me about you," Skye continued. "You apparently had him rolling with laughter. You should really think about getting into showbiz; we need more talent." Skye talked so easily with Jayna. "Also, you can call me Lucy, that's what my friends call me".

"You need more talent in showbiz and in the hair industry too. Ohhhhhh!" Again, Jayna's hands flew up in the air because she couldn't resist the chance to roast Elle again.

One of the artists was trying so hard not to laugh; then it suddenly erupted out of her mouth, spilling noise out into the hallway. Elle was laughing now with tears puddling in her eyes.

"What is all of the racket?" Prina's head appeared through the door. "Wait … what? Wait … what?" Prina was absolutely starstruck after seeing Skye.

"I always have that effect on people," Jayna deadpanned, pretending that she was the one who had Prina awestruck.

The entire room erupted with laughter again.

"Skye, this is Dr. Prina Patel, who is one of my dearest friends and helped coordinate our visit here today. Prina, this is Skye Reynolds." Elle was able to finally get control of her laughter and properly introduce her two friends.

"How is it going today with our makeup team?" Elle asked Prina.

"I believe the team is just finishing up, but I would love to get some photos with your team and with Skye if she is willing," Prina mentioned.

"I am not sure because I don't want to give anyone the wrong impression of our effort here today," Elle shared.

"I understand what you mean, but it would be a great memento for the families of the kids here. Plus, it may be a great memento for the team too," Prina said.

Elle looked around the room, and everyone was either smiling or nodding in agreement to Prina's words.

"I have to admit that I think most of you will want a photo of me before I become a world-famous actress or hair stylist. You will want this memento," Jayna teased.

Before she knew it, everyone in the room was huddled together for a series of photos.

As the team packed up their supplies, everyone said their good-byes to Jayna and the other teens. Elle leaned over to Jayna with a serious expression on her face.

"How much longer will you be here?" Elle asked Jayna.

"They said a few more days, but maybe sooner if I keep healing at this pace. I hope it will be soon. I am so ready to get back to my fans in my neighborhood." Jayna couldn't resist the urge to joke.

"Since Jesus is our homie, I'll keep praying for you, ok?" Elle smiled.

"I have been praying for you too. I know you seem like you are doing all of the things, but I think you are still a little nervous, and that is ok. God's got you." Elle hugged Jayna after hearing her kind words. Elle was afraid she would tear up if she didn't give her a hug.

Elle had the team meet at the entrance of the hospital to debrief.

"Thank you so much for coming here today. You all made me so proud seeing you open up your hearts and talents to these kids. You gave them hope and some distraction for a few hours. I am asking that you get back to the fashion house in an hour so we can get back to work. Also, text me your coffee or tea order so I can get some-thing delivered to you this afternoon when we return. We have some final work to do. Does anyone have any questions?" Elle asked.

"I have a question." Jayson raised his hand and began talking at the same time. "Why did we come here today?" Jayson was teasing Elle because he knew the reason but wanted to ask just to tease her. Much to Elle's surprise, different members of the team began answering the question.

"We came to give back to someone else."

"We came to share our talent."

"We came to help give us purpose."

"We came to help us become a better team."

"We came to work better together."

"We came to practice our skills and have fun."

"We came to remember our purpose is bigger than just a fashion show." Jayson answered his own question.

Elle's heart was about to burst when she heard the responses from her team. "Does anyone else have any questions?"

"When can we come back to visit the hospital again?" Devan asked with a wide smile on her face because everyone was thankful for the unexpected visit.

Chapter 26

"Do you have time to go to lunch with me? I can make it a quick meal because I really want to spend every minute with you that I can until..." Liam paused. "Until ... after the show is finished." Liam couldn't say what his heart was thinking. He had never fallen so quickly for someone, never felt like he had known her his entire life.

When thinking of Elle, Liam had so many conflicting feelings. In some ways, he had become so jaded with the people in the world of show business, and Elle had been unlike everyone else. He struggled with pangs of guilt to even consider that he may move on with this relationship, almost feeling selfish. If he chose to pursue a relationship with Elle, he had to come to terms with feeling like he was leaving his sister on her own. His sister, who trusted just about anyone, would be all on her own. However, he had given up years of his life, a life he left behind to protect his sister. Could he move on now? Could he leave his sister? Could he leave Elle? Liam's thoughts were flooding his mind.

"Absolutely," Elle answered back. "I would love to go to lunch with you."

"I didn't know if you were feeling like you had too much to do before the team arrived back at the fashion house. Don't feel like you have to say yes," Liam admitted.

"I am not stressed about the work ahead of us for the day. We have the dress rehearsal tomorrow, and I just need to keep my team working together. How do you think the hospital visit went?" Elle asked, hoping to get some reassurance with what she thought she saw.

"You are amazing. I could watch you working with the kids at the hospital all day," Liam almost whispered and stepped closer to Elle.

"Well, I meant how did you think my team did with the kids, but I won't complain if you are inspired to come a little closer to me." Elle slid one hand behind Liam's neck and used the opportunity to close the gap of space between them.

"Hi," she whispered and brushed her lips so softly against Liam's cheek, allowing her nose to brush against his nose simultaneously. She left her face against his for a moment in an embrace, taking in his woodsy scent and the warmth from his breath. Elle had never been one for public displays of affection, but there was something about Liam that made her want to hug and kiss him, but she didn't want to have their first kiss there.

As if on cue, Elle's phone began buzzing just as Liam put his hand gently on her cheek.

"I am sorry, but this is Margaux. She was heading back to the fashion house to set up some things for me so I have to get this." Elle stepped away from Liam while still hanging onto Liam's hand.

"Oh my gosh Elle, oh my gosh!" Margaux was doing her usually overly excited squealing.

Normally, this would have sent Elle reeling with anxiety, but she knew Margaux was excited about something.

"What's up?" Elle was smiling at Liam while beholding the phone to her ear.

"Our hospital photos are going viral. I mean the world is going nuts over the photos of the kids with a sneak peek from the show's style. I keep seeing people comment…" Margaux was thrilled with the possibility of being among the famous.

"Wait … what do you mean? How are those photos going viral? I thought they were for the families? Are you saying that those photos have been used as a marketing tool by someone? They used what we did for someone's good as a way to promote the brand?" Elle's voice was shaking now. She dropped her hand and stepped away from Liam. Elle started pacing because her mind was racing.

"I am coming to the fashion house. I have to set this straight. I am furious that someone would use this visit to promote the brand. Don't get me wrong; I know what we have been hired to do, but the hospital was not part of this package. I'll be right there. Our team doesn't need to think that is why we did this. I know I shouldn't have trusted people to do the right thing with the photos." Elle was ranting and pacing at the same time.

Liam was watching her while completely confused by the change in her demeanor. He picked up the gist of the conversation but couldn't believe that Elle would even be surprised by this happening.

"I can't do lunch now. I have to get back to the fashion house and set things straight. Some self-promoting jerk used our time at the hospital to further their brand or their own agenda. I can't stand dealing with some people in this industry. You can't trust anyone. I'll just take an Uber." Elle was already on her phone ready to get the Uber.

"Whoa, whoa, what is happening? I'll take you back to the fashion house. I get what you are saying about the industry, but you can trust me. I'll get you back now." Liam tried to offer reassurance, but there was an awkward silence hanging between them and Elle was consumed with putting out this proverbial fire.

Elle was talking to herself now. "Why did I let anyone take a photo? Who shared the photos? Why didn't I have Prina take the photos only instead of allowing everyone else to take photos? Why didn't I know that someone would use this as an opportunity to promote themselves? Why am I not surprised that someone would do that very thing I was trying to prevent with our visit to the hospital? I can't trust anyone."

Elle's thoughts were swirling, and Liam was taking in all of the things she was saying to herself. Liam realized that Elle was not wrong about most of the people in this industry, but he was discouraged by seeing her so distraught by this small thing. She hadn't felt the weight of this industry yet. He was quietly driving and giving Elle time to vent, watching her in the back seat absolutely consumed by her frustration or possibly anxiety with what had transpired so quickly.

"Why did I agree to this job? I've made a huge mistake. I should have just stayed in New York and paid back my parents for the next five years. My dad was right. This industry is full of fake people; I can't take not trusting people." Then the dam broke. Elle was sitting in the back seat crying; this was where the stress of the show hit her and the weight of balancing everyone was on her shoulders. She only *thought* she had it all together. This betrayal was just a reminder of control only being an illusion.

Liam pulled the car over and parked for a minute.

Elle was still crying and didn't notice the pause on the ride.

Liam turned around and took her hand. "I am so sorry you are dealing with this, but if there is anyone who can turn this betrayal into something beautiful, it is you. I would like to add that I am so thankful you took this job, even if you see it as a mistake," Liam almost said in a whisper. With that, he turned around and resumed his drive to the fashion house.

Elle could feel the weight of her actions and her words and shame hit her like a brick.

They pulled up to the fashion house, and Elle was at a loss for words.

"I am just going to drop you off here. Text me and let me know what I can bring you for lunch. Let me know if you need anything else," Liam said in a somewhat distant manner.

"Liam…" Elle paused because she couldn't think of words that would make things right. "I'll text you in a bit," she lingered as she was wavering about what to do to him. She wanted to apologize for how she acted, but she didn't want to begin crying in frustration in front of Liam. She had to go see the team and make sure they understood the truth behind their visit.

Elle walked in the door and could tell that Margaux had been in tears.

"Margaux, I overreacted about the media posting. I am sorry if I betrayed your trust by what I said. We do need to address the fact that I didn't have us visit the hospital to promote the Axel Scott brand, or Skye Reynolds, or even me. I wanted us to connect as a team and be the hands and feet," Elle continued.

"I get it. I know you aren't in the throes of social media, and I understand how this may have caught you off guard. However, we have work to do, don't we? I don't think it will change what the team felt after spending some time there. Truly, I don't think that some social media comments will change what our team felt in their hearts after connecting with the teens," Margaux said reassuringly.

"I hope so. Let's get some supplies ready for the team to arrive so we can start our work as soon as they arrive back." Elle went to one of the storage rooms.

"Cheers!" echoed throughout the room after she opened the door to get the supplies. Elle was shocked by the entire team hiding and cramming themselves into a tiny storage room.

"What is happening?" Elle looked confused.

"I know you said we could go get lunch, but we wanted to do something for you. We bought a traditional English tea set-up." Jayson was beaming.

"We do have something to celebrate with the world going nuts over the looks you created at the hospital," Elle said, expecting a resounding yes by the team.

"What are you talking about? Did people like our looks on social media? We just wanted to surprise you because the hospital visit was a great reminder for the real purpose of our work, and it is amazing to think that we could help someone feel a bit better. It's just a proper thank-you and a proper English tea. Cheers!"

Devan began setting up the food and tea for the team to enjoy. Elle and Margaux said cheers to the team. The group squeezed together for a group photo. Elle was so grateful for this moment and for the reassurance of her purpose today. She knew she overreacted and knew she overreacted with Liam too. She had to make things right with him.

Elle stepped aside and tried giving Liam a call, but it went straight to voicemail. Elle's heart sank, knowing that she didn't blame Liam for not taking her call.

Chapter 27

Elle was exhausted by the end of the day. She and the team planned, redesigned, timed, made adjustments, and worked well into the evening. Elle's brain was getting fuzzy from leading, making decisions, and planning, but she still felt the urge to check her phone for texts from Liam. She refused to get distracted with expecting a call or message from him after the way she behaved over the social media leak.

"Are you ready?" Margaux asked and helped return Elle back to the here and now.

"I think we are good until our dress rehearsal tomorrow. I have to say that I am so proud of the team today. How do you think it went?"

"I was shocked that you fired Alyssa immediately, but I understand that you had to make her an example too. I mean, I have never seen you so stern before, but I understand that you had to establish yourself as the lead stylist too." Margaux trailed off, almost seeking an explanation on the unexpected behavior.

"About that … I meant to tell you about it before it happened, but it was an idea I had late last night. I'm sorry I didn't tell you. Alyssa was a hired actress; I didn't fire her. It was all a ruse so that I could set the tone for the collaboration among the team. I honestly didn't know if I would actually need to fake-fire her, but once I arrived and heard bickering among the team, I was thankful I planned the coup," Elle explained.

"Wow, next time, please share it with me ahead of time? I didn't know what to do for a second. What would you have done if the team was 'playing nice' when you arrived? What would you do with an actress who doesn't know how to actually do the work? I am impressed with your ability to plan that far ahead for building your team. I am always learning from you for sure, even if I didn't know how to react. You are always so surprising, Elle. I mean that in the nicest way, so don't fake-fire me too," Margaux deadpanned.

"I would have had her leave and not return. I was thinking I would just secretly ask her to flake out on the job with an unexpected emergency or go to the bathroom and not return. I was warned by Callum that many of these artists can be very rude, competitive, and demanding, and I wanted to set the tone for our work. This is such a short amount of time with each other and such a short window for planning that I didn't want to deal with competitive egos. I am sorry that I didn't warn you. I didn't know if it would all come together honestly. But I am so thankful it worked."

"When is Liam coming to get us?" Margaux asked as she, too, was beginning to look tired after the long day.

"Actually, I haven't heard from him so I may call an Uber. I was incredibly rude to him today when I found out about the social me-dia post, and it made me question everything and everyone. I just went off, and I was so angry and thought I may have inadvertently directed my frustration at him. I feel awful about it and tried to reach out to him, but he isn't answering his phone. If he isn't here to pick us up, I get it. Let's head out and we can call an Uber. Let's lock up."

"Ladies, ladies, you are still here?" Both women jumped after hearing the voice.

"Oy! You scared us, Callum!" Margaux cried.

"Sorry dahling, but you aren't the only ones who need to work late tonight. Dress rehearsal tomorrow, and you know Axel is going to be here with high expectations. From what I have seen, today was a good day. By the way, who thought about taking the team to a hospital for a day of service when you have the show to prepare for … but then again … Axel Scott has never given full control to a lead stylist for a show. Axel called me into his office about the stunt," Callum stated without any indication, if the comment was compliment or a complaint.

"Oh Callum, I am so sorry that he may have gotten upset with you about our little trip today. It didn't occur to me that he was going to have an opinion about it as long as it didn't affect our work. I hope you didn't have to take any responsibility for my actions. I feel terrible about my oversight," Elle apologized.

"Dahling, I didn't say he reprimanded me. I just said he called me into his office. I didn't say anything about him being angry … he was thrilled about the additional media exposure and the fact that you represented the heart behind the project. He wasn't upset that his brand received some additional positive press, but he was most impressed with the service and community you created by the little stunt," Callum said with a mischievous smile.

Elle's heart felt lighter and felt slightly touched by the compliment.

"Do you want to go out for a drink to celebrate our good day, dahlings?" Callum requested.

"I am going to pass because my brain is so fuzzy right now, and I just need some down time tonight. Margaux, what are you planning to do?"

"I am happy to go out with you, Callum," Margaux confirmed. Suddenly, Margaux appeared to have regained her energy level, and she was truly there to experience all that she can during her visit.

"Again, no police this time … please. I'll see you back at the hotel." Elle hugged Margaux and Callum goodbye. Just as they were leaving the fashion house, Elle recognized Liam's car parked across the street, and her heart raced just a bit to see it. Elle quickly headed in the direction of the car while practicing her apology in her head.

Elle approached the car as Margaux and Callum headed in the opposite direction arm in arm. Elle loved that Margaux seemed to be hitting it off so well during their work here and smiled to herself, knowing that Margaux was checking off ten things on her bucket list since moving to New York while coming on this trip.

Aside from work, Elle didn't know too much about Margaux's personal life. She knew that Margaux moved to New York City from a small Midwest town just a few short months ago. Margaux didn't seem to have many friends if at all in New York, so she seemed to have jumped right into work to keep her busy. Elle smiled, thinking that Margaux had made a friend with Callum during this trip, and she had genuinely enjoyed getting to know her more on this endeavor. Elle thought to herself how you usually see someone's true colors during this kind of work, and Margaux had been nothing but professional, encouraging, and hard-working.

Elle continued walking toward the car and gently knocked on the window. She was a little surprised because normally Liam would be out of the car, greeting her, and opening the door. She was thinking about how mad he must have been about Elle's behavior earlier that day. Elle heard the doors unlock and was surprised to see Lucy sitting behind the wheel when she opened the door.

"Hello there, beautiful," Lucy nearly sang as she greeted Elle. Elle absolutely loved Lucy's positive and kind demeanor, but was a bit crestfallen that it wasn't Liam sitting behind the wheel.

"Oh my gosh, what an amazing surprise. You drive?" Elle was unsure if she should hop in the car with Lucy driving, wondering if it was even safe.

"Of course I do! I just prefer to be the passenger princess when I can. Can I give you a ride back to your hotel?" Lucy asked. She was holding back laughter by Elle's surprised reaction that Lucy could in fact drive.

"Absolutely, but I am sorry you felt like you had to be my driver. You know I could have taken an Uber. Is Liam ok?" Elle tried to sound casual while asking.

"He said he had something come up and couldn't come to get you. He was really weird about it too. Then again, my brother can be annoying and pretty vague from time to time so I am not surprised. He said he had 'something' most of the afternoon today, so who knows. Do you need to get any food on the way to the hotel? You may need to get out if you want the food because people tend to get a little crazy when they see me in public. So, there is that." Lucy giggled like her situation was an everyday occurrence for everyone.

"I am actually good and don't need anything to eat. My team bought me a traditional English tea today for a little surprise."

"Wait? What?" Lucy looked surprised.

"My team surprised me today after we went to the hospital when we returned to the fashion house. They wanted to make sure I had a proper English tea, so they surprised me with a nice, little spread," Elle said with a smile. "We all snacked on it most of the day today. It was a huge spread and such a sweet surprise. They were ador-able with their excitement in surprising me," Elle said, smiling while thinking about the afternoon with the team.

"That is so bloody nice and surprising," Lucy said as she pulled onto the street. "This industry can be so competitive, and usually teams don't take time to show so much kindness to each other, es-pecially with such a short amount of time together on this project. Wow, I am just … wow. I knew you were good with style, but Elle, I didn't know you would be such a master lead stylist and so strategic at building a cohesive team. You are truly great at your job and hilarious too … I might add, which is the real box-checker for me," Lucy joked.

"Well, it is difficult to balance my hilarity with my job, but I think I can manage," Elle quickly responded. "We could have our own comedy show if you ever get tired of making world-famous movies." Elle heard Lucy laughing.

"By the way, thank you so much for picking me up. Tell me about your day," Elle requested, as if she and Lucy were old friends. It was so easy to talk to her, and Elle wanted to take the focus of the conversation off of her.

"Well, I went to the hospital with this amazing team of talented, kind-hearted people and met some absolutely brilliant kids. I think that was the highlight of my day. I read a potential script and dodged some paparazzi. I did a bunch of nonsense the rest of my day. I had to get fitted for some clothes for a fashion show and was pampered a bit too. I admit though that the hospital visit was the highlight of my day, except for now. I had the distinct honor of driving an in-demand lead stylist and hair icon so that is a close second," Lucy deadpanned.

"Can we hang out after the show? Literally, you are the funniest person I know. I need to laugh like this all the time … every day," Elle said, while wiping the corners of her watery eyes from laughing at Lucy's dry delivery.

"I think we may need to plan a fun girl's weekend when you are finished with the show. We are literally hours away from Paris. Wouldn't that be perfect to do a girls' weekend?" Elle's heart fluttered thinking of the opportunity to have a girls' weekend and secretly hoped that Liam may be the person to drive them there. That is if he hadn't completely given up on whatever they had going on between them, Elle reminded herself.

"Lucy, can I ask you a question about the night we met?"

"Are you wondering what happened that night?" Lucy made eye contact with Elle. "Well, I decided to surprise the guy I was seeing before going to my movie premiere event. He lived near your shop.

When I arrived, he was with another woman. The thing was, I wasn't really mad at him; I was mad at myself about it. There were so many red flags that I ignored because I didn't want to believe the truth. I saw the light on at your shop and just knocked on your door." Lucy smiled, revealing how thankful she was for meeting her.

"Thank you for sharing that with me, Lucy. I am sorry that happened to you." Elle began getting out of the car after they arrived at the hotel. Elle was pleasantly surprised that Lucy was actually a decent driver. She assumed she was hell on wheels because she never drove herself.

"Should I plan to take an Uber in the morning? Is Liam still going to be busy?"

"I don't know; you should ask him," Lucy replied.

"I tried reaching out to him today, but I haven't heard back, and I don't want to be a bother to him. I mean, I don't want to bother him if he had a thing today."

"You should just ask him." Lucy was almost insistent like she knew more than she was letting on with Elle.

Elle went on to repeat what Lucy was clearly not understanding … Liam was not answering her texts, but she continued, "I haven't heard from him today, so should I just text in the morning?" Elle was surprised that Lucy didn't seem to understand that Elle and Liam hadn't talked most of the day, and her insistence was making Elle feel even worse about the situation.

"Thanks again, Lucy," Elle started to say as she was closing the car door.

Just as she was about to close the door, she heard Lucy say, "Just ask him because he is standing right behind you."

Chapter 28

Elle turned her head slowly to see Liam standing with his hands in his pockets, looking rather shy while waiting in front of her hotel. He looked sheepish, almost like he was hiding something. Maybe this was the look he had when he wanted to break up with someone. Was this something that would necessitate a break-up? Regardless, Elle was really excited about seeing where this thing would go at this point, and she hadn't dated anyone in years, or ever, that actually made her excited about the prospects.

"Hi there."

"Hi."

Elle wasn't sure what to make of Liam's appearance, but she was not afraid to apologize. She knew the power of feeling so much shame and having some of the unkindest words spewed at her by her demanding and hard-to-please parents. Her time in medical school fueled the words of doubt and the habit of constantly proving herself still plagued her from time to time now. She craved not only a kind word or encouragement, but hoped for an apology when their demanding words crossed a line and fell into being cruel.

"I need to say something," Liam began.

"If you don't mind, I want to say something first. I am so sorry that I was so rude, and I overreacted. I have issues with trusting people sometimes and … and what I said wasn't directed at not trusting you. I was just frustrated at the situation, and I feel like I directed that frustration at you. I. Am. So. Sorry." Elle stood in front of Liam while he was standing with a hard-to-read expression.

There was silence as the two stood looking at each other. Elle felt the need to fill the silence with even more words.

"I am not making excuses, but I have been around some very hard-to-please parents for most of my life. I have learned to try to do things on my own, and I have a hard time letting go. I have a hard time trusting people, and I am sometimes overwhelmed with…" Elle had to take a moment to take a deep breath to keep control of her emotions. "I am sometimes overwhelmed with the fear of disappointing people, and the way I acted today was me allowing that doubting voice in my head to take over. I really do try to do better, but today, I didn't. Again, you didn't deserve it."

Again, Liam didn't speak. Anxiety was beginning to creep through Elle, so she filled the void with more words. "Can you say something because even if you hate me forever, I would at least like to know if you hate me now so I can stop rehearsing in my head how awful I treated you today?"

"I had a thing today," Liam said quietly.

"Lucy told me that you were busy, but I will be honest, I thought it was code for I-don't-want-to-see-that-over reactive-woman-again 'thing,'" Elle said.

"Lately, I have been thinking about my job and wondering how much longer I want to keep doing this," Liam began in a subdued voice. "My sister seems to be doing better in her life. I don't feel like I have to protect her as much as I used to do," Liam continued.

Elle's stomach sank. He had been moved to quit this job. The job that he took so that he could be closer to his sister. After all these years, he was considering leaving his job now that he had had to work with her … Elle the tyrant. She was feeling awful about his words and felt the burden of guilt on how this would impact Liam's sister.

"I don't feel like this is something I want to keep doing because I need something different in my life. This job doesn't fulfill me," Liam continued. "I had a job interview today. Actually, I had a second interview today too."

"That's great for you if that is what you want. I am happy for you if you are ready for a change. I just hope that I haven't been the reason for your need to leave your job."

"You really are to blame for me looking for something different," Liam replied with a hard-to-read expression.

Elle's eyes grew wide, and she was speechless, paralyzed by knowing what to say to Liam at that moment. She was good at questioning herself and his words were like a stab to her heart. She normally would fill the void with words, but she couldn't come up with anything to say.

Liam grabbed her hand so gently. "You are absolutely the reason I want something different," he said in a tender whisper.

Elle looked confused. "So, you don't hate me for the absolutely awful way I spoke to you today?"

"I couldn't hate you. You have inspired me to want something for myself for the first time in a very long time," Liam said softly to Elle.

"You deserve to have the job you want," Elle replied, paused, then asked. "What is the job you want?"

"Elle, I am not talking about the job; I am talking about wanting YOU," Liam stepped closer to her and took her other hand into his hand while gently rubbing the backs of her hands with his thumb and looking into Elle's eyes.

"So, the thing you want is me?"

"You could absolutely say that." Liam almost whispered as his lips brushed gently across Elle's mouth.

Elle couldn't hold back anymore. She held Liam's face in her hands.

Liam whispered, "I was hoping for a more romantic place, but can I kiss you now."

Elle just nodded; she couldn't speak … words escaped her.

As they stood under the soft glow of the streetlights in front of the hotel, Elle could feel her heart racing, her breath coming in shallow gasps. She looked into Liam's eyes, searching for any sign of hesitation but only found a mirrored intensity, a longing that matched her own. His hand brushed against her cheek, tentative yet reassuring. She felt a shiver run down her spine as he leaned in, his lips brushing against hers in a whisper of a touch. Time seemed to stand still as their kiss deepened, a silent promise of things to come.

Breathless and aware of the very personal moment they just shared in such a public place, Elle's mind returned to reality.

"What job did you interview for today?" Elle couldn't remove her arms from around his neck, as she was eager to see what direction he was thinking of going.

"I had a Zoom interview today for a job in New York City in the financial district. You see, I met this girl, and she makes me want to spend more time with her. I feel like I have known her my entire life. I admit, she has a bit of a temper, but she seems to have a good head on her shoulders. Did I mention that this girl lives in New York and the idea of her leaving in a few days has me rethinking everything about my life?" Liam revealed the boyish grin that charmed Elle the first time she felt a connection with him.

"I didn't think you liked the financial work you did previously. I love the idea of you coming to New York, but I don't want to have you take a job you would hate to come to New York. I care about you too much to have you take a job you hate."

"Well, this isn't doing at all what I used to do previously in New York, and I think it is a perfect challenge. Plus, it is near a girl that I really, really like." Liam stepped even closer to Elle.

Elle pulled her arms tighter around Liam's neck and brought her hand up the back of Liam's neck, gently massaging it. This time, she brushed her lips against his.

"Funny, because I was wondering how I was going to say goodbye in a few days to a guy that I really, really like too," Elle admitted to Liam as he brushed a hair away from her face. She was so thankful to have him in her arms after the guilt she felt earlier today. She didn't want to say goodbye to him in a few days either or maybe even ever.

"Why didn't you tell me about your interviews?"

"I was going to tell you today, but your little temper reared its ugly head, and I didn't think it was the time at that moment." Liam was teasing her now. "After seeing your temper today, I thought you may have been a robot because you were so perfect. Now, I know you are a real person. Plus, I would like to take some time to work on our relationship with you, even if it means we argue from time to time." Liam was brushing Elle's face with his thumb as his hand settled gently on her cheek and he looked into her eyes. His look penetrated Elle's soul.

"Yeah … I really need to work on that temper. Thank you for giving me a second chance. I am a changed woman because I don't want to mess up what we have going here."

"After meeting you, remember when I snapped at you the first time we met? I think I can give you some grace on your bad moments. We both have them. I admit though, you make me want to be a better man. There isn't anyone else I would rather fight with, to be honest," Liam said and pulled her even closer to him.

Elle and Liam were in a close embrace when they heard some applause. When they turned around, they saw Lucy who had been waiting in Liam's car.

"I am so happy to see that the lovebirds made it through their first argument. Now, who wants to go out for breakfast in the morning?" Lucy shouted from the car.

Chapter 29

As suspected, Elle woke up especially early the next day. She had her outfit ready for the "dress rehearsal" for the show. Today was the only day they had to get the kinks out of the show's pace. She was so thankful for Liam and Lucy's invitation for breakfast to help start her day off right. Plus, Elle could get very busy at work and forget to eat from time to time, so this was the perfect idea to at least help her get some food in her stomach today.

"Hello, beautiful." Liam pulled Elle to him as she approached him while he was leaning against the car holding two cups of coffee. He no longer tried to make their relationship a secret. He brought his mouth up to Elle's cheek, giving her the gentlest kiss and whispered, "You look phenomenal. You are going to do amazing today. I couldn't be prouder of the work you have done over such a short amount of time. You are the real deal," Liam whispered in her ear while holding her close to him.

"You are very good for my ego, good sir. Honestly, I am really not that nervous about today. I just know it is going to be a lot of work and adjusting our plans. I just hope that Axel Scott is agreeable and not too prickly about the show. I put enough pressure on myself, so

I don't need him to put more pressure on me too," Elle said honestly.

"Well, let's go get Lucy and get a proper breakfast so you have the energy you need for your big day."

"You didn't pick her up first?"

"You see, I wanted to spend every moment that I can with you, so I opted to get you first. Is Margaux riding with us?"

"No, she and Callum had a late-night last night and responded with a firm 'no' for breakfast. I told her I would get her some food and bring it back for her at the fashion house. She is going to set up some things for us before I arrive too."

"Wow, look at you and your boss-lady plans." Liam opened the door for her.

"You know I can sit up front at this point since we are actually spending some time together. You are more than just a driver to me. I can't hold your hand from the back seat," Elle tried to convince Liam.

"I won't complain about the handholding, but I know that you and Lucy will want to catch up the moment you see each other, so I think the back seat will work best to let my two favorite ladies spend some time together too."

"Good point. You and your sister have quickly become my favorite people," Elle shared with a hopeful smile. Elle's heart fluttered when thinking about Liam's words describing Elle and Lucy as his two favorite girls. What a sweet guy to speak of his sister and his potential girlfriend like that.

"You, aside from that temper, are one of the best people I know," Liam teased her.

Both Liam and Elle smiled at each other through the rearview mirror, allowing the silence to say what both of them were thinking.

Elle sipped her coffee that Liam had ready for her in the back seat. She was thankful for her busy schedule because she didn't want to think about the logistics of their relationship. It would be ideal to have Liam near her if he did take the job but didn't want him to feel pressured to leave everything he knew there too. Plus, she was really going to miss spending time with Lucy.

"Hello, beautiful," Lucy cooed as she got into the car after they arrived.

"Hello, dahling." Elle attempted her best effort at recreating a stuffy British accent.

"I have to tell you something that you may or may not love. I just want to tell you straight away," Lucy said with clear apprehension. "Here it goes," then Lucy said the next part as fast as she could. "Axel-Scott-will-be-joining-us-for-breakfast." Lucy sat there with a nervous expression, waiting for Elle's response.

"Are you looking like that because of my newfound reputation of having a fiery temper?" Elle tried to make light of the sinking feeling in her stomach after hearing that Axel Scott would be joining them. "It's fine. I mean, he is the fashion designer, and we are about to have a big show tomorrow so I could see where he wants to meet with us. I just didn't know it was a working breakfast. I was hoping for a little rest and relaxation before today, but it is ok, really."

"He asked me when we could chat today and I told him we

were meeting for breakfast, and then he invited himself." Lucy even squirmed while saying that. "He is a really nice guy, but he can be a bit … much." Lucy's eyes grew wide, and she had an annoyed expression on her face. This was a fact that Elle could understand based on the little interaction she had had with Axel.

They arrived at the restaurant, and Elle could tell immediately that this was an exclusive place. There appeared to be two layers of security to arrive inside the door, a place to see and be seen. Although this wasn't as opulent as dinner. Elle took in the rustic charm of Field to Fork when they arrived. She could see that the restaurant offered only the freshest, seasonal ingredients for the most exclusive customers.

As they finally entered the separate private dining room, Axel waved the group excitedly to the table. Elle was surprised that he arrived first compared to his usually late arrival to the fashion house.

Axel greeted their group with cheek kisses as so many Europeans do. "If it isn't the rock style icon, Skye Reynolds," Axel cooed. "You. Are. Rocking. It," Axel said as he held onto both of Lucy's hands.

Axel gave Liam a wave, then turned his attention to Elle, who began to squirm because Axel seemed almost chipper to see them. "You are like a seasoned professional, Elle. It has been an honor to work with you so far. I know today is the day that is going to be the true test of our work together, but so far, you have been a pleasant surprise to this industry," Axel said with such sincerity it nearly caught Elle off guard, while she was still trying to determine if his welcome was actually heartfelt.

As they took their seats, that was when Elle noticed the extra chair. Places like this would not leave an empty seat at a table, with the exclusive tables being filled with other patrons. Elle thought to herself that Callum may be joining them. In that case, she thought, she wished that Margaux would have been invited because it almost seemed like a working breakfast. That's when Elle saw a new face approaching their table.

"Hello there, I am Imogen Larison. It is a pleasure to meet you." She held out her hand to only Elle; it was clear that Imogen must have already know everyone else at the table.

"Imogen, I am so surprised you are here. I thought you were on assignment in Ukraine. What brings you here to London?" Lucy asked with a surprised expression on her face, appearing to clue Elle in on the fact that she didn't know about this extra guest. Even Liam appeared to be surprised by the guest.

"Actually, I finished my work and decided to come back home to London for a few weeks. Then, I started hearing about this up-and-coming lead stylist who has a heart of gold and is blowing up on social media recently. And I wanted to learn more about this woman of mystery." Imogen smiled in Elle's direction. "I mean lifestyle and entertainment is much different than my usual work, but I couldn't pass up the opportunity to meet you."

"Is this an interview? Are you a reporter?" Elle tried to hide her annoyance with what appeared to be a coup. She knew that people were always looking for the next big thing in style, and this type of thing was common in the fashion world, but she didn't even know she was on the radar of anyone. Elle wondered why Imogen said Elle was "blowing up social media" when she didn't even use it.

"Let me be honest. We don't have too many up-and-comers take the world by storm with an iconic makeover, leading a style team for a fashion icon, and now we learn she has the heart of an angel. The world needs to know more because you are an inspiration. Think of the young stylists that can learn by your example. You may be bringing the heart to an industry that has been known to be heartless." Imogen was convincing with her words. "That is why I am here. After seeing families destroyed by war over the past few weeks, I need a story like yours." Imogen's last words were almost a whisper, and Elle could feel some compassion for the writer, despite this meeting seeming pre-planned and partly a marketing ploy on behalf of Axel Scott, Elle suspected.

"I don't really do things for attention or for recognition," Elle said weakly and clearly felt uncomfortable with the unwanted attention.

Imogen's smile widened as though she was waiting for a moment to hear a story about a person like Elle.

"That is what I have heard about you … and I think the world needs to hear more," Imogen offered as almost a reassurance to Elle.

"Elle is an icon. She has been in the hair world for a few years, but it is a funny story how we met." Lucy was much more comfortable with opening up to Imogen. Elle wondered if Lucy knew more about Imogen, which made her open up more in such a short amount of time. Elle also thought Lucy may have been protecting Elle by offering her a story. "The night we met, I had been seeing a man, who shall remain nameless, for a few weeks. I decided to surprise him at his apartment in New York before heading to my premiere. I caught him with another woman so I decided to skip the opening night event and get a new look from Elle that night. She came up with my rocker style as you already know, and she and I became fast friends. She is special and lovely, and I am so glad she has become someone very special to me." Lucy grabbed Elle's hand in a reassuring and appreciative way.

"Lucy, I mean, Skye is what everyone else calls her, reached out to me after the world went crazy about the lead stylist job. I am not on social media much at all, so I had no idea who Lucy was when I did her style." Elle smiled at Lucy as she shared the story with Imogen. Elle was starting to relax a bit after talking about meeting Lucy.

"Wait … you had no idea Skye Reynolds was one of the most coveted actresses when you gave her the new look?" Imogen was taking notes. "This is so great. So, what made you decide to take the leap into this line of work after having your own salon in NYC? Did you do something before hair? What led you to this world?"

Elle was frozen. She did not lie but didn't want to share the painful truth with a stranger. She didn't want to share her past with the world; this was so painful to talk about, and she didn't want to come off as some emotional mess. Elle's life verse came to her mind. "You have no obligation whatsoever to do what your sinful nature urges you to do." Elle took a deep breath while the entire table watched her expectantly. Elle's heart was flooded with peace after mentally speaking that verse, her life verse, as her pulse slowed and her demeanor changed. This was the moment she decided to let go of the regret of her past. Regret that she carried for years without reason. A lie that she believed over years but had come to learn that it was all smoke and mirrors.

She changed career paths and was discarded so easily by her family that she was convinced by the lie that she was worthless for too long. She was no longer carrying this regret, and for some reason, now was the time that she truly realized it. Elle was amazed at God's timing of all places to feel the weight of regret lighten in the middle of a crowded restaurant and in front of a reporter.

Liam touched her hand gently because he could easily see Elle was struggling, but with what, he didn't know.

"I took the job because I owed my parents a lot of money." The table grew quiet, and the tone of the morning turned a bit serious. "I used to be a medical student and decided to change my career to being a hair stylist after having a special connection with a young burn patient during my internship. I styled this girl's hair, and the pure joy she experienced during that short time we were together put into perspective what really mattered to me. I no longer wanted to be in the world of competition with medical students vying for the perfect internship and trying to impress their professors, but I wanted to see the immediate fruits of my labor by doing hair.

"I left medical school. My parents shut me out of their lives and insisted I pay them back for medical school within a month of leaving school. I took this job because I will finally be able to pay off my parents quite frankly. Plus, Lucy asked me to do the work, and I loved the idea of hanging out with her a bit because she is absolutely hilarious, and I had no idea she is as famous as she is until now, really. I love what I do, but that was my intention initially in taking the lead stylist role." Elle smiled reluctantly, but honestly.

"I second that. She found her new bestie, and we can spend more time together," Lucy joked, which Elle was appreciative of the joke, given this personal moment that she had shared.

"This makes sense about your visit to the burn unit. Did you want to help like you did in medical school?" Imogen inquired.

"I always try to serve in the burn units whenever I can. I do it in NYC too. This type of service brought me to my true passion. One of my dearest friends is actually doing her residency in London so she helped me get our visit coordinated. It was not meant to be a publicity stunt. So, let me be clear: I wanted to take the team to the burn unit because they needed to be reminded of what really matters before doing our show. From what I have learned in this short time in this industry, this business can be a competition among colleagues like my medical school experience. My team needed a reminder of their true purpose before we started our work together. The hair and the clothes are only the tools to help our clients discover who they really are.

"Take Lucy, I mean Skye. She just needed a reminder of the rock star that she is, and the hairstyle was just the reminder," Elle said smiling at Lucy, and Lucy appeared to almost be teary-eyed.

"I have to admit. If this show is as successful as the critics are saying, you may be one of the most sought-after lead stylists in the industry. Would you consider staying in London if an opportunity arises?"

Elle didn't say anything but smiled widely at Liam.

"I am learning that there is so much to love here in London," Elle replied while making quick eye contact with Liam. Lucy beamed while seeing Liam and Elle staring at one another. She began to realize that her brother might be falling in love.

<h1 style="text-align:center">Chapter 30</h1>

After an early breakfast, an impromptu interview, and a long day at the fashion house, Elle was thankful to be leaving for the night. Given the demands of the day, the surprise interview at breakfast seemed like another day. Elle smiled as she saw Liam leaning against the car as she left the fashion house. She ran to him and gave him an all-consuming hug, inhaling the woodsy smell of his cologne and burying her face in his neck. Her pulse slowed, and although he couldn't see it, a smile spread across her face as she nuzzled Liam's neck.

"I think I can get used to this," Liam whispered into her neck. Liam was just about six inches taller than Elle so she could easily wrap her arms around him. Neither of them moved, remaining there, hugging one another. Elle's heart was racing just being so close to Liam, but her body wanted to take in this moment.

It was Liam who stepped away first. "What can I get you? Do you need food? Do you want some coffee? Wine? What would you like?" Liam was so sweet and attentive after Elle's most important day so far on her job.

"Food would be good. Thank you for reaching out to see if I

needed anything today, but I just didn't even feel like I could stop for a moment to eat. I am game for takeout and a nice quiet evening in, if that is ok? I haven't been to your place yet. Before we go any further with this relationship, I need to see this status of your place. I mean, if you still have your mattress on the floor, this may have to be a no-go regardless of your charms." Elle paused with a concerned look as though Liam's mattress might actually be on the floor.

Liam teased Elle by pretending to be horrified by Elle's comment and suggesting by his reaction that his mattress may actually be on the floor.

"Please, please, please tell me your mattress is not on the floor," Elle pleaded after making the joke.

"What is the deal with the mattress on the floor? What is wrong with the floor?" Liam attempted to defend himself while still having a college-like apartment. Liam's smile widened, as if leaving Elle in suspense had gone far enough. He didn't want her to have any reason not to come to his place. "I do not have my mattress on the floor. Are you planning to see my mattress tonight?" Liam joked, and Elle's face turned bright red, not realizing the direction this conversation would turn.

"You said something about food." Elle tried to change the subject because she wasn't even close to begin thinking about that type of relationship with Liam.

"I have the perfect little Indian restaurant on the way to my place. Thankfully, I just took my mattress off the floor in the event you decided to come over to my place," Liam joked again. "I can cook you something if you like. I can actually cook at my age. I make a great homemade spaghetti sauce, but it may take a little while if you are really hungry. Would you like me to cook for you?"

Elle's heart fluttered a bit just seeing the hopeful look on Liam's face when asking if he could cook for her. She still couldn't believe that this attentive, smart, loyal, gorgeous guy who drove around famous people hadn't found a special someone with a lot more zeroes in their bank account than Elle currently did. How was she sitting in the same car as this amazing guy right now?

"Raincheck on the pasta sauce because I am famished. I would love to another time though. Maybe sometime soon? I could destroy some paneer curry or tikka masala. What is your favorite Indian dish? We could share something if you like. Honestly, I may eat your meal too. I just realized how hungry I am now that we are talking about the possibility of eating." Elle's smile widened as if she needed food like pronto.

"I just put in our mobile order," Liam said as he set his phone aside. "I tend to overdo it when I have people at my house. I want to impress you and make sure you have anything you like." Liam smiled. "I had a feeling you would mention Indian food because you haven't had it since you mentioned it a couple of days ago, so I took the liberty and ordered everything." Liam grabbed Elle's hand and gently kissed the back of it.

Elle took in the neighborhoods as Liam drove them to his place. He parked in front of a classic place in the Notting Hill neighborhood. It was old but well-kept and stately. His place stood out among the rest with its bright green door.

"I love the curb appeal of your place, but we forgot to get the food." Elle looked at Liam a bit concerned.

"The restaurant is just a three-minute walk. I am going to get you settled in my place, and I can run to get it. Come on in," Liam smiled as he unlocked the door.

When Elle walked in, she could smell his familiar woodsy smell. She was greeted by a friendly Orange Tabby who said hello and rolled back on its back, exposing its belly. "Well, hello, sweet baby, what is your name? Ok, how have we not established that you have an adorable cat?"

"That is Coco." Liam's smile widened.

"Wait, like my Coco fur baby?" Elle was teasing. "There is no way that we both have cats named after Coco. I mean, what are the chances?" Elle was stunned.

"I will not confirm or deny the roots of my fur baby's name," Liam deadpanned. "Why haven't you mentioned being a cat dad before now? I mean, you know I have a Coco in my home already. This is really weird." Elle was shocked to see this adorable cat begging for attention at her feet.

"Well, we should think about getting the kids together with my Coco and your Coco ," Liam joked but made Elle's stomach flutter when thinking about the possibility of the future of their relationship being an actual thing.

Liam attempted a quick tour of his home. "This is my living room and if you continue up these steps...you will find my kitchen."

Elle took in the contemporary look of the living with the Midcentury Modern touches without being too overstated. Liam had warm colors throughout the space that felt so cozy, yet sophisticated. She followed him up to the kitchen and took in another inviting room. It was clear that Liam had great style. His kitchen had modern appliances and cozy, warm-colored cabinets. He had a small bistro table in the kitchen with a formal dining table in an adjacent room. Elle was taken in by the sophisticated charm of the space when a growl broke the silence.

"Was that your stomach growling?" Liam asked, and Elle's face turned a shade of crimson.

"Yes, it was, I am so embarrassed. I think just being in the presence of a kitchen reminded me that I need food," Elle said awkwardly.

"This tour is cut short until I get you some sustenance. Let's get you seated right here in my living room. Check out the view from that window. It is quite lovely. Also, put your feet up here. I am going to grab you a water before heading to pick up the food." Liam appeared to enjoy taking care of her. Liam brought the water and was out the door to pick up dinner.

Elle smiled to herself as she took a slow sip of water, feeling absolutely content with sitting in Liam's home. She hadn't felt so taken care of like this before in her life. Her parents were always a bit formal ... even in their own home. There was never much warmth in her home as a child. Plus, Elle hadn't dated much either. She dated another medical student for a short time, but he was much like her family— very formal and a bit standoffish. Liam was almost doting, and everything about him exuded warmth.

With her feet up on the coffee table, Elle looked around the living room and couldn't resist the urge to explore Liam's place more. She continued up the stairs to the kitchen and dining area. Just off of the kitchen was a set of stairs that led outside, and Elle's curiosity got the better of her again. Elle climbed the steps and realized the stairs led her to a rooftop terrace with an absolutely stunning view of the Notting Hill neighborhood. She looked over the edge of the wall and saw the beautiful trees that outlined the charming neighborhood. The terrace must have been one of Liam's favorite places because it had a welcoming well-worn L-shaped sofa that hugged a gas fireplace. The terrace had a border of greenery that surrounded the entire rectangle shaped space. Edison bulbs zigzagged across the patio area and illuminated the area once Elle found the switch. The night had a crispness but was actually ideal in what was commonly rainy London. Elle walked around the perimeter of the space and looked over the greenery to see the streets and other patios or gardens spotted throughout the area.

She couldn't believe she was standing in an apartment of a man she had really grown to like after such a short time. These past two weeks had been a whirlwind. Elle sat down on the outdoor sofa and took in the beauty of this little slice of heaven. She was smiling to herself when she had a sense she was being watched.

"Sorry to just watch you, but I love seeing you so relaxed here. You found my favorite spot in my home." Liam appeared with two very large bags of food. The smell made Elle's stomach start growling again. "Would you like to eat up here? I can start the fire and grab a blanket," Liam offered.

"That sounds lovely. What can I do?" Elle stood up.

"I know you've had a long day, and I would love to give you a break," Liam reassured her. He placed the food on the table that sat near the sofa. He turned on the fire, then started some quiet jazz music. "Here you go and here you go." Liam set out all of the food and explained each dish he purchased. He wasn't kidding when he said he overdid it by purchasing too much food.

They both began feasting and sampling the food. Elle dug into the tikka masala and offered Liam a bite. His smile widened when he noticed her gesture. Gathering all of her favorite items on her fork, she held up the perfect bite, and Liam opened his mouth, allowing just a small drop of sauce that landed on the side of his mouth. She brushed off some sauce, noticing that Liam loved the gesture. It took everything she had not to grab his face and kiss those sweet, soft lips, despite having sauce smeared on the edge of his mouth.

"I am so glad that I met you," Liam said with a serious face. "Really, I have never met someone like you." Liam's honesty with his feelings made her feel so thankful for a guy with integrity and honesty.

"I was just thinking the same thing. I couldn't help thinking how did a guy like you give me a chance. I mean, you must have met a hundred beautiful women driving for your sister. I am sure you have had women throwing themselves at you." Elle too wanted to be transparent. "I am just not like that world," Elle said, as though he may find this fact a disappointment.

"That is one of the things I like about you. You are not like the pretentious people that I have met through my current job. You aren't like anyone I have ever met … ever. I am thirty-one years old, and I am done with fake people. I have been hoping for years to meet someone real, not like my coworkers in the financial sector or the pretentious people that my sister works with daily. I kept hoping for someone," Liam paused then continued. "I didn't realize it until now, but I have been hoping for someone like you." Liam sat for a few seconds completely quiet and lost in his feelings. He took on a tone of confession. "I feel so bad about how rude I was to you when we first met, but I hope you know it was because of the people that are usually in my sister's circle. She often trusts the wrong people and until I got to know you, I was worried about my sister. You have such integrity about your work and how you live your life. You inspire me to be a better person and a better man." Liam took her hand and kissed the back of it again.

"You make me feel so awkward with such openness and honesty, and especially after I destroyed most of this food you bought," Elle attempted a joke so that he wouldn't keep throwing compliments her way. Elle had never been able to receive compliments very well.

"Let me clean up some of this food," Elle stood up, and Liam was quick to take the bags from her hands.

"Allow me." Liam took the bags from her hands and called over his shoulder as he walked down the stairs, "Feel free to adjust the switch on the fireplace, and I will be back with some wine."

Elle was soaking in the evening tonight. This was perfect; it was a lovely meal and a perfect evening. The fireplace offered just enough heat to take the chill out of the late summer air.

"Here you go." Liam offered Elle a glass of wine and sat next to her on the sofa with his arm snuggled gently behind her.

"I could get used to this." Elle smiled and put her head on Liam's shoulder as they both watched the flicker of the flames.

"I wanted to ask you something, but you don't have to talk about it if you don't want to," Liam continued.

"Sure." Elle lifted her head and shifted so that she was facing Liam.

"What are you going to call your invention? Do you even call it an invention? Patent? Do I call it a cream? What are you going to call it? You seemed a little hesitant or I just didn't know if you didn't have a name for it yet," Liam asked not to be pushy, but to get to know her better. "You just seemed hesitant to share that before, or maybe you don't know what you are going to call it?" Liam asked and gave Elle's hand an encouraging squeeze, then took her hand into his.

"Actually, I have a few different ideas in mind, but I think I have narrowed down my ideas. I think I plan on calling it Milk and Honey," Elle smiled awkwardly, waiting for Liam to look confused by her response.

"I love it. Is that like the land of 'Milk and Honey'? Is that a Bible reference? I think I remember something about the land of milk and honey. Is that what gave you your inspiration for the name?" Liam asked with genuine interest.

Normally, Elle would squirm a bit when referring to her faith. Most of the time, people don't know what to think about Elle or what she was saying about her faith, but with Liam, she felt comfortable opening up about it. She noticed that Liam seemed to have an interest in learning more about it.

"Remember when I mentioned that my parents cut me out of their life when I decided to leave medical school? Well, I always thought my parents were model Christians. I admired them. They volunteered and signed up to help in various charity and service events. They really became leaders in my Christian bubble as a kid. When I left medical school, I saw my parents in a completely different light. The supportive Christian people I once knew were gone. My dad especially surprised me because we were so close and just one day, he didn't want to speak to me or couldn't even make eye contact with me. When they shut me out, it changed the way I saw them and their faith.

"So, back to the name of the cream I created, I want the name to reflect the promise of a better life for those who use the product. I hope that it gives them a second chance. Yes, the title comes from the Bible when the enslaved Israelites were given a chance at a free life. Secretly, I hope that one day my parents may see the product and give me a second chance too. I hope they realize that I can still help others and use my medical knowledge even with my new career path. I can still serve as a Christian doing what I do now; it doesn't just have to be in medical school." Elle's lip began to quiver so she reached out to grab her wine glass for a sip to help her collect herself because she didn't want to ruin this evening by getting emotional about her past.

"I grew up with such an unconventional life, and I didn't grow up with church or even Christians in my life. If you are how Christians are supposed to act, you inspire me want to learn more. I just have never known too much about it." Liam's smile seemed almost uncertain. Elle really loved how easily he shared his feelings. He wasn't shy about sharing what he was thinking while most didn't know the truth, let alone speak it with subjects like faith.

Elle took his face into her hands and slowly put her lips on his. She kissed next to his mouth slowly and kissed the opposite side of his face. She placed a gentle kiss on his eyebrow, peppering his face with soft, gentle kisses. She gently rubbed her thumb slowly on his face.

"I can definitely get used to this," Liam whispered.

Elle shifted on the outdoor sofa to sit even closer to Liam. She could smell that familiar woodsy smell. She put her feet up on the rest just in front of her and took a deep relaxing breath. "I could get used to this too," she whispered back, and a rush of contentment came over her.

Liam and Elle sat entranced by the fire, snuggling next to one another, and Elle could begin to feel the drowsy feeling of a full stomach hit her. Being the first time to slow down for the day, Elle could feel a drowsy sensation become even weightier.

A loud noise came from the adjacent flat, and it startled Elle. "What was that and what happened?" Elle was completely confused and staring bleary-eyed at Liam. She realized she must have fallen asleep while snuggling up against Liam. Even Liam's eyes looked red like he had fallen asleep, and his hair looked a little disheveled too.

"Bloody hell," Liam stood up in a rush apparently as confused as Elle.

Elle and Liam both started laughing and realizing they both fell asleep on their perfect date once they snuggled up to one another while relaxing by the fire.

"I better get going with my big day tomorrow," Elle said as she began to stand and gather her things. "I'm so sorry I fell asleep during our date. It was perfect. Really, it was lovely."

"Why don't you stay?" Liam asked her while holding out his

hand and pulling her closer to him. While holding her in a warm embrace, Elle nestled her face into his neck and could feel her body relax again. She didn't have to leave, but she didn't know what Liam might want if she would stay. Liam put his lips near her ear and whispered, "Stay," and Elle smiled to herself, wondering if she should follow her head or her heart.

Chapter 31

The next morning, Elle kept smiling to herself as she was thinking about last night while she was getting ready for her day at the hotel. She tried to focus on her day ahead, but her mind kept taking her back to her romantic evening at Liam's flat. Despite only getting a few hours' sleep, she was alert, and her brain wouldn't stop going from the details of the fashion show to the perfect evening last night.

Elle heard a gentle knock on her hotel room door, opened the door, and saw a bleary-eyed Margaux standing in front of her, handing over an oat milk latte.

"You, my dear, are a lifesaver. How did you know I needed fuel this morning?" Elle uttered.

"Actually, I woke up a little early when I heard your door this morning. If I didn't know better, I think you just arrived back here just an hour ago. I thought you may want some coffee if I did in fact hear you just get back to your room," Margaux teased Elle without pushing her too much.

"You would be right … I do need the coffee." Elle purposely

avoided giving Margaux more information about her whereabouts last night.

"Oh man, you are killing me. I love a good romance story, and I would just like to hear the deets of the amazing time you and Liam had last night. I mean, I don't want THE details because that would be icky, but I would like to know what you are thinking about your relationship at this point." Margaux said the last part with a bit of a squeak, while simultaneously walking past Elle and sitting cross-legged on her bed.

"You aren't going to make that tea kettle sound when I tell you details, are you?" Elle asked.

"It depends. Did you like the tea-kettle sound? If so, yes, I can arrange that I squeal like a tea kettle," Margaux deadpanned, but made a circular motion with her hand to prompt Elle into telling her some details.

"He. Is. Amazing." Elle didn't even attempt to hide her feelings for him. "He is such a romantic kisser. He is thoughtful and protective. He is hard-working. He is a bit of a caregiver and so attentive. He is smart, wants to be a better person, and wants to grow in this faith. I am actually excited about the possibility of seeing where this thing may go, and I have never felt this excited about a guy in … well … ever," Elle admitted.

"Good kisser, huh?" Margaux hinted at wanting to know some real details by moving her eyebrows up and down in a sup-posed-to-be-flirtatious-manner.

"Actually, I fell asleep after dinner," Elle smiled.

"Wait … what?" Margaux looked confused and slightly stunned

by Elle's honesty.

"He picked me up and took me to his flat for dinner after work yesterday. He offered to cook for me, but I was famished and didn't want to wait for food. We ordered takeout from a little Indian restaurant near his flat. We ate on his terrace, which was so charming and beautifully decorated. It was perfect." Elle had this feeling of contentment wash over her, and she paused for a moment, enjoying the memory in her mind.

"I am confused … where did the nappy time come into play because I thought you had the perfect night. Sorry, is that what you consider a really nice date?" Margaux asked.

"Well, after dinner, I had the after-dinner heaviness hit me in a big way as we watched the fire while snuggling on his outdoor patio. We were listening to some jazz music and sipping some wine. I was so relaxed just talking and snuggling that I fell asleep. We both actually fell asleep," Elle said, shrugging her shoulders like falling asleep was the most normal thing anyone would do on the world's most romantic date.

"I am even more confused. How did you find out he was a good kisser? Did you dream he was a good kisser?" Margaux joked and was pleased when her comment made Elle laugh out loud.

"Well, after we both woke up from our little two-hour siesta, he asked me to stay at this flat. Yes, there was some kissing and hugging, but there was so much talking, planning and learning about each other. I feel like I have known him my entire life. It is so easy to talk to him. He said what he wanted most last night was just to get to know me better," Elle said nonchalantly.

"So, he wanted to 'know' you better, huh? Did that include…?" Margaux hoped for juicy romantic details, but Elle quickly stopped her. Again, Margaux kept making ridiculous movements with her eyebrows, also breaking out in some goofy shoulder dance moves.

"He was a perfect gentleman. He wants to start going to church with me too. After our little nap, we talked almost all night, and it was perfect. I feel like I have known him so much longer than I actually have. It is so strange. What time is it? Oh gosh, I have to finish getting ready." Elle reminded both of them that she had to focus on one of the most important days of their professional lives.

"This relationship is getting real if you are using I-feel-like-I-have-known-him-my-entire-life-bit," Margaux teased.

"Is that something you have personally experienced or are you like a love doctor?" Elle knew that turning her comment back on Margaux's love life would shut down the teasing, even if Elle didn't really mind it.

"A little of both quite honestly, but we have to get ready to head out for the day." Margaux was finally on board to tackle the day. Margaux stretched out her legs and hopped off the bed and began heading toward the door of Elle's hotel room. Elle noticed that Margaux was quick to change the subject when the conversation turned to her love life. Elle noted that Margaux seemed to really avoid any love conversations, all joking aside. She just began to realize that Margaux hadn't dated as far as she knew before moving to New York, and she never talked about anyone special, so she was surprised by her reaction when the tables were turned on her.

Margaux quickly responded, "After all, I am sure you haven't figured out all of your relationship details after the show concludes," saying this just as she was about to head out the door.

The look on Elle's face was all the information that Margaux needed to know that Elle and Liam may have actually made some potential plans for their relationship.

Margaux was frozen in her tracks before walking out the door. "Wait, you guys actually have talked about what happens next? Are you engaged?" Margaux asked with almost a demanding tone.

"No, I am not engaged, but he may be moving to New York," Elle said nonchalantly.

Margaux bounded back into the room and embraced Elle with the tightest celebratory hug, and that was when Margaux's tea-kettle squeal began to fill up the small hotel room.

Chapter 32

Leaning against the car with his beautiful smile on his face, Elle saw Liam waiting outside that hotel to take her to the fashion house. He was holding Elle's favorite coffee blend in his hand, and she didn't have the heart to tell him that she already had more than enough coffee this morning. She didn't know if it was the big day, the coffee, or just seeing Liam again that made her feel electric.

"Good morning, beautiful." Liam handed the coffee to Elle and brought her close for a morning hug. Elle could feel his warm breath on her neck as he nuzzled up close to her. He whispered encouragement in her ear, "I am so proud of you. You are going to be amazing today." I can't wait for the world to see your talent." Elle felt a surge of reassurance fall over her, and she took in the encouragement and the tenderness that Liam seemed eager to share with her. Instead of avoiding it, she took it in with a thankful heart.

Liam opened the door for the back of the car, but Elle again insisted on sitting next to him so she could hold his hand.

"As I am sure you know, I brought Margaux to the fashion house about an hour ago. I texted her to make sure there weren't any last-minute items that she needed. I also took the liberty of getting her some coffee too. I hope I got her order right. Anyway, I am going to drop you off and run some quick errands before this show begins. Message me if you need anything at all. I will come straight away to help." Liam kissed the back of Elle's hand as he went on with the day's plans. "Does that plan work for you? I can stay at the fashion house if it will make you feel better having me nearby in the event you need anything," Liam continued.

"Your plan sounds perfect," Elle continued. "Thank you for always being so kind and thoughtful about everything. I would never expect you to put your day on hold while we get ready for this fashion show. I do appreciate it though," Elle said with the most tender expression. "Really, I appreciate all that you have done for me." Elle really meant more than just all the driving and thoughtful coffee deliveries. Liam brought a softness to Elle that she didn't realize she needed in her life.

When they arrived, the fashion house was buzzing with life. Flowers were being delivered, and teams of people were coming and going as Elle entered the door. She almost felt like she was running late because of all the excitement and activity in the fashion house, but she knew she was an hour early. Americans keeping much earlier hours in general than most Europeans was a fact that Elle learned quickly during this trip. The people at the fashion house now were the behind-the-scenes workers and service workers that were preparing for the show.

Elle was absolutely in awe at the decorations flooding the entry. Fresh flowers have been delivered, but they were not the dainty flowers but instead carefully curated displays that reveal rock-and-roll influence. Black, red, and white blooms covered the entry and walkway as Elle arrived, and the sweet scent of flowers gave just a hint of fragrance without being overwhelming.

"Text me if you need me. Otherwise, I will see you soon," Liam called out the door of the car while Elle remained at the door of the fashion house. Elle was brought back to reality when she heard his voice. Until that moment, she was just taking in the splendor of the decor.

"Thank you." Elle ran back to the open window and grabbed Liam's hand one more time and leaned down for a quick kiss. "See you soon," she whispered.

Elle turned back to the fashion house and attempted to not be so impressed with the initial design of the space. At this moment, she felt like the country mouse in the big city. This was where the experts showing their talents were celebrated. This level of opulence was not at all what Elle had ever experienced, despite living in New York City. This was unchartered territory for Elle.

While working here, Elle learned that Axel Scott's fashion house was a working fashion house. Much of the fashion designs were completed in house in the upper levels of the building while the lower level housed space that would allow for Elle's team to work as well as host the fashion show. Axel Scott didn't produce many designs that were similar, but instead created a chosen few designs in specific size. More sizes would be made later, but it was a select few attendees who could take one of the ready-made designs home after the show today, which made them even more exclusive. This level of quality radiated everywhere today. Elle knew that a really successful show would not only sell on-hand items, but also have multiple orders after the show.

Exploring the space, Elle saw the "Heart of Rock of Roll" fashion logo subtly embellishing various items. The logo was being projected on the floor as she entered the long hallway that led to the back of the building where the runway was located. Elle took some time to explore the space now that chairs were in order, decor was being placed, and the final touches were being put into place throughout the venue.

Elle walked down the hallway and could see the hors d'oeuvres and cocktails being set up for guests as they arrived. A DJ was setting up to play rock-n-roll house music. Elle continued down the hall to see the hidden kitchen area that was used for the chef to set up and prepare the small bites. Elle continued walking to the back of the building where more rock-themed decorations were being placed from ceiling to floor without being overdone. Elle could see more working spaces as she continued down, working her way to a carefully designed runway in the back of the building. An actual tattoo artist was setting up, which absolutely shocked Elle thinking that someone would decide to get a tattoo while attending a fashion event.

Finally, she made it through the entry to the runway area. Sofas, which were the first row of seats, had been placed facing the runway. Each decorated intentionally to support the rock theme of the event. Swag bags had been placed with the names of people who were seated closest to the runway. Lighting had been brought in to reveal the rock theme too; the logo was projected in various places on the floor. An additional DJ station was set up back here as well near a food and drink area. Elle laughed when she saw the charcuterie skewers that were carefully placed like a mohawk on a mannequin's head. There were so many details celebrating the theme. Elle took it all in and couldn't believe that she was standing here as a lead stylist.

"This is unreal, isn't it?" Elle heard a voice whisper nearby.

"I know! I am trying not to look so in awe at everything," Elle said to Margaux and walked up and joined hands with her. Both women stood holding hands while taking in the room, almost as though they were grounding each other in the moment.

"I can't believe we are here," Margaux said with her usual excitement.

Elle squeezed Margaux's hand in a thankful and appreciative way that said everything she just couldn't say in that moment. She showed how thankful she was to have Margaux by her side for the past few weeks in New York, but to also have her experience this work with her. She was beyond thankful and humbled that she could be used like this for her work; this exceeded any dreams she ever had of doing her work.

"Are you ready?" Margaux asked Elle.

"I think so, but I want to do something first," Elle said, "Let's go back to our work space."

Elle and Margaux went to the style area where the team would be working for the day.

"I know we haven't done this much together, but I feel like I need to pray over our work together today. I usually pray personally, but not usually with anyone else. Do you want to pray over our work today together with me? You don't have to do it if you feel uncomfortable," Elle said.

"Girl, I am from Indiana, and we pray about everything from hunting season to Friday night football games. I would love to pray over our biggest workday of our lives," Margaux again joked, but her honesty helped Elle feel more at ease.

Both women stepped aside in the style room so that they could have a private moment for their prayer. Margaux held out her hands to hold Elle's hands again so they could bow their heads and face one another as they prayed.

"Lord, bless our work today. Help us use our talents to celebrate and love others. I want to thank you for having Margaux in my life and for her work she has done for this project. Although I should be teaching her as she is new to our industry, she has taught me just as much as I have taught her." Margaux gave Elle's hand a thankful squeeze. Elle continued, "I ask that you bless our team today. Thank you for bringing each person to this team. Thank you for revealing their kind hearts when we served at the hospital. Thank you for allowing them to love on us as they treated us for tea." Elle could feel a hand rest on her hand on her shoulder. Elle continued with eyes closed, and her head bowed, "Thank you for helping each of us find our gifts so that we may glorify you through our work." Elle felt a hand on her other shoulder.

Elle continued again, "Lord, help today run smoothly and help us encourage one another. You have blessed us beyond measure, and we thank you," Elle finished and opened her eyes as she was eager to find out who joined their prayer.

Much to Elle's surprise, she found her entire team encircling Margaux and Elle for the prayer. Elle didn't know what to say and was so thankful that they joined them in prayer. She didn't know if any of them believed, but here they were, a ragtag team of people giving God all the glory, and Elle felt so humbled by this moment.

"Thank you so much for joining us in prayer," Elle said to the group.

"Are you kidding me? The moment I heard you praying and thanking God for me and my dusty self, I had to join in on that prayer. I don't hear too many people feeling thankful for me," Jayson joked, but his true appreciation was shown in his face.

"Group hug," Margaux shouted and suddenly Elle found herself completely squished in the middle of the funniest, most obnoxious, and sweetest group hug of her life.

Chapter 33

The style team had finished prepping for the show, the models had arrived and were ready to go to the runway. The team was just waiting to be given the green light. Even Lucy was all set, being the big inspiration for the show. She looked stunning. She wasn't going to be the first person to enter the runway but one of the last. Her style was going to be part of the big finale.

Axel had been surprisingly hands-off, and Callum had returned one more time before the show was to begin in less than thirty minutes.

"Hello beauties. Elle, where is your expertly designed outfit for today?" Callum asked.

"Wait, I have my own outfit to wear today? Something designed for me?" Elle looked shocked. Elle looked to Margaux for clarification on how she may have missed this information. Margaux looked like she was clearly in on the secret.

"Oh gosh, I had no idea. I don't know what to say. Thank you. I mean, thank your fashion team for doing something so kind for me. I'll go change. I am so excited that I have an Axel Scott design of my own." Elle started moving to a changing area with excitement.

"Oh dahling, Axel purposely wants to surprise you with a little something. He wanted to surprise you, but he will never admit that he was being kind. So don't even bother saying anything to him. I put the design in the changing area there. Go change, then Bob's your Uncle, we will be ready to go." Callum was smiling from ear to ear.

Elle entered the changing area and put her hands on the delicate black material. There were black combat-style boots in Elle's size. The black slip style silk dress cascaded down the hanger. There was a black net-style top that covered the top half of the slip dress. The top had black pearl embellishments that were strategically placed on the design. In small letters on the tag was written, *Elle, you are the heart of rock-n-rock —Axel Scott.* Elle was completely taken aback by the beauty and delicate design of something that was feminine, yet the embodiment of rock-n-roll.

It took Elle a few minutes to put on her outfit. Inwardly, she was starting to feel a little stressed because she doesn't do last minute very well. She paused to maintain her composure and not let anyone know she was getting a little anxious with these last-minute surprises. At this point, she was hoping to just sit around and chat with the team while they waited to be given the green light. Elle thought she heard someone say her name.

Elle shouted behind the curtain, "I'm sorry, Callum, I couldn't hear you. Give me a second" as she was sliding the curtain open.

In a louder voice, and with his ringed fingers cupped around his mouth so that his voice could be heard, he repeated, "I said you have one more person to do hair for."

When Elle left the changing space, she saw Jayna standing in front of Callum with an excited smile.

"So, I heard that you guys needed me for a finale in the show," Jayna said, being her usual sarcastic self.

Elle nearly ran to Jayna and gave her hands a big squeeze. "How are you here?" Elle asked, while being completely thrilled to see her.

"Long story, but I have been released to go home. I heard this show needed someone to really bring the house down in your finale, so I offered my services," Jayna joked.

"Jayna!" Another voice could be heard in the room. Lucy entered the room and approached Jayna while they both simultaneously did a secret handshake that looked like they had rehearsed it.

"I am so happy to see you and hear that you are out of the hospital. YOU are going to bring down the house today! This is such a brilliant surprise; let's get you runway ready!" Elle took Jayna's hand and led her to her styling chair.

As Elle was finishing up with Jayna sitting in her chair, she took in the room. The stylist team was ready, Jayna and Lucy were joking non-stop with one another as Elle worked, and Margaux and Callum were chatting in a corner. Elle knew this team would only be together for these few short days, but she was so thankful for this ragtag team that brought her so much joy during her time here. Elle noticed that there was only one person missing … Liam.

"There you go, sweetheart; you are ready," Elle said to Jayna, and finally Jayna took a look at herself and had tears in her eyes. For just a few seconds, Jayna allowed herself this moment to be vulnerable. She was so thankful to feel beautiful after not knowing if she would feel beautiful ever again. With her lip quivering, Jayna whispered, "Thank you."

Then, Elle noticed the entire team was standing around Elle when she finished with Jayna, and they began clapping. Elle didn't know if they were clapping for Jayna or for the beginning of the show. She didn't care; she was so thankful for all the encouragement that the team was giving one another.

Callum entered the room and said what they all have been waiting for, "We have the go!"

"Let's go bring down the house," Jayna shouted, and the team lost all composure and began cheering and hugging one another and ran to their places.

Chapter 34

The show was a whirlwind. The team was organized and ready, but it was a constant flow of people, communication, movement, and changing.

The team was ready for their last movement, and Elle noticed that she still hadn't seen Liam yet. I know she told him he didn't need to be around here all day, but she thought he may be around at some point today.

It was time for the finale, and Lucy was positioned to make her entrance.

Elle could hear the music change in preparation for her entrance, and the crowd cheered as Lucy entered the runway. Lucy walked the length of the runway, showing full confidence with her shag haircut and expertly designed clothes.

She returned momentarily to the stage area, then walked down the runway again, but this time holding hands with Jayna. Jayna was smiling from ear to ear and waving her hand with her free hand.

The style team was huddled together and watching all the stage action from the screen in the changing area. The team anticipated this moment. They were smiling and watching the crowd respond and cheer for Lucy and Jayna. The group stood watching the screen, some holding hands with one another and some with their arms around each other in support. Elle and Margaux were standing along the group, but Elle secretly still couldn't help but notice that Liam was still not anywhere to be found. Perhaps he was watching the show, she wondered.

The music changed as Lucy and Jayna finished their walk and returned backstage. Small flames illuminated the stage to indicate the finale. The applause could be heard back in the style area from the runway. Inspired, the style team continued the cheers not only for Lucy and Jayna, but also for themselves and the hard work that had been done this week.

The group could see Axel Scott enter the runway with the models, and he took a microphone to thank the patrons for their support. He asked for the style team to join him on the runway. After saying a few kind words, Axel asked Elle to join him up front.

Axel Scott took Elle's hand as he held the microphone with his other hand. "I want to thank Elle Bennett for leading the style team. She made my job very easy this week, and she also inspired this show. She gave Skye her famous new look, and she also has a heart of gold and the heart of rock and roll too." Axel smiled and waved Elle up closer to him. "Please put your hands together one more time for Elle Bennett and her team."

Of course, Elle waved the team out to join her up at the front of the stage. Applause continued to fill the room.

"Elle took this amazing team to a local hospital to do some mini-makeovers with some teens in a burn unit. Our feature model,

Jayna, is one of the newly released patients. Please give our model, Jayna, a hand," Axel continued to give such a heartfelt speech at the conclusion of the show, which was almost surprising to Elle.

Axel continued, "This is just the start—."

That was when Elle saw Liam sitting in the audience smiling from ear to ear. She smiled back and gave him a wave, but then, that was when she saw Liam's guest. Elle walked away from the stage as Axel Scott was speaking and stepped down into the audience without thinking. Axel watched, almost speechless, because he was unclear what Elle was doing while he was still thanking her for her work. Axel watched Elle as she walked to Liam and the man sitting next to him. Liam's guest stood up and met her halfway. They both embraced in the middle of the crowd with all eyes on them. The crowd was captivated by what was happening.

Embracing him, the familiar citrus, soap smell came to her, and she was reminded of learning to ride a bike with him pushing behind her. She remembered him helping her with her science project when she was in elementary school. She remembered him teaching her to cast a fishing line on a church trip. She remembered the satisfaction she felt when she knew she made him proud. Elle was embracing her dad who came to her fashion show. Liam had brought her dad to her fashion show, and as Elle and her dad both embraced one another and sobbed, even Liam watched with tears in his eyes.

Meanwhile, the entire fashion show team, the audience, and even employees working the event were in tears. No one knew who Elle was embracing, but they were witnessing such a tender, emotional moment that they couldn't help being touched by these two people embracing. Even Axel, who was initially slightly perturbed by her walking off stage, could see that she was emotionally shaken by this surprise. Everyone who witnessed this moment knew they were witnessing something special.

Suddenly, Elle remembered being in the midst of a fashion show. Liam handed her some tissues. She looked around at all the teary eyes on her that shared her moment. Her dad whispered, "I know we have a lot to talk about, but you need to know I love you and I am so sorry." Elle's lip quivered again as she let go of her embrace. She hugged Liam as a thank-you and made her way to the runway.

"I am not sure what we just witnessed, but Elle, it looks like you just had an amazing surprise," Axel said without expecting a response. Wiping her eyes, Elle nodded without saying a word but smiling a teary smile. "Well, ladies and gentlemen, thank you for coming to our show. If anyone needs tissues or a drink after our unexpected finale, feel free to help yourself to items in the back. Thank you for all your support and love. And keep rocking!" Axel said, raising a glass of champagne with rock-themed decor embellishing the glass. Suddenly, servers appeared around the room and lively rock music filled the space. The team on the runway began dispersing, hugging and greeting, and moving around the room.

Elle returned back to Liam while her dad was getting himself tissues and a drink in the back of the venue.

Elle was shocked. "How did you do this?"

"I wanted to see if I could help mend some pieces to my girl's broken heart," Liam confessed. "I didn't know if it would work, but I wanted to try. I hope you don't mind that I reached out to your dad, but I do have one more surprise for you," Liam smiled.

Chapter 35

Liam took Elle by the hand and led a very confused Elle across the room trailing behind him, while snaking through the crowd. With Liam's wide shoulders and tall build, she couldn't really see where they were headed, but again she flooded with gratitude. As they continued their walk weaving through the crowd, they stopped with well wishes and congratulations as they made their way across the room.

Elle was shocked by the number of people who thanked her or shared a special moment with her as Liam attempted to lead her across the room. Again, Elle had such a feeling of gratitude fall over her. Sure, she had a great deal to discuss with her father, but for him to be here was amazing. Her Dad apologized after he could barely be in the same room after she decided to leave medical school. She couldn't believe the effort Liam took to help mend the relationship.

"Elle, you are a rock goddess!" Prina hugged her friend.

"Wait, you were in the audience for the show?" Elle asked while simultaneously grabbing Prina for a hug.

"I wouldn't miss it for the world. Plus, Elle, oh my goodness, you and your dad! I can't believe he is here. I can't believe he complete-ly surprised you to come to the show. Elle, this was so special." Even Prina got a bit teary-eyed and paused to compose herself a bit.

"Who knew that a fashion show would make most of their at-tendees cry?" Cliff put his hand out to shake Liam's hand and then drew Elle in for an awkward hug.

"She is the heart in the heart of rock-n-roll," Liam deadpanned.

"Nicely done, my love." Elle high-fived Liam for the bad joke.

"If you will excuse us, I have a little surprise for Elle," Liam smiled wryly.

"If you don't mind, we are going to pretend we aren't going to follow you to said surprise, but we are going to follow you to the sur-prise," Prina smiled with confidence.

Liam led Elle again with Prina and Cliff following them across the room, all four joining hands while snaking around the crowd. They approached a small group, and Elle couldn't see anything else other than the backs of the people who were standing in a small circle in front of Liam.

"Excuse me, Cece I have someone I would like for you to meet." Elle could barely hear Liam say to someone standing in front of him who again couldn't be seen due to his wide hulk size blocking her view.

"Lovely to meet you. I heard of your talent a few weeks ago, but what I have come to adore more is your kind heart. My team made me look good today until you bloody made me cry during the show. Was that your father?" Cece held out her hand and greeted Elle like she was a familiar friend.

Suddenly, Elle realized that THE Coco Lush, also known as Cece apparently, from THE band, Femme Frequency, was standing in front of her very own eyes! Coco Lush, Cece, as Liam called her, was also one of the most influential fashion designers as well.

Liam began realizing that Elle seemed slightly dumbfounded regarding who was standing in front of her. "As you already know, this is Elle Bennett, who is one of my biggest inspirations and one of the best people you will ever meet." Liam smiled while widening his eyes, as if to clue Elle that it was time for her to speak.

Elle could hear Prina whispering from behind her, "That's Coco Lush. That's Coco Lush. That's…"

Elle finally began. "I am so sorry. I didn't realize you would be here for the show. It is such a pleasure meeting you, and thank you so much for your support. It is an honor to have you heard with your fashion influence and big heart yourself. I hear you are always making a difference in different groups you are involved with too," Elle said more confidently. "I am sorry to sound rude, but did Liam call you Cece?" Elle again started feeling like her usual wise-cracking self.

"Liam has called me that since primary school. I was a few years older, but we knew the same people. He knows how much the nickname drives me crazy," while she poked Liam's arm. Elle just marveled that Liam's circle was so wide, and he was one of the humblest people Elle knew.

"Back to you making me bloody cry, my team and I were discussing if it was a pre-planned stunt, but I said no. Did you mean to make everyone on the show cry today, Elle?" Coco said teasingly.

"I have to say that I would not have broken out into the ugly cry in front of a room full of some of the most influential people in London for a stunt," Elle said sincerely. "Instead, I prefer to break into the ugly cry in my bedroom or during a shower without the audience," Elle deadpanned.

"She is witty, talented, and quick, Liam. Are you sure you've got it in you to keep up with this kind of lady? I mean, once she hears your primary school nickname, she may decide she needs to find another bloke," Coco teased Liam like a sister would joke with a brother.

"You are right. She is completely out of my league, but I hope she doesn't notice. Let's try to keep that a secret." Liam smiled at Elle.

"Elle, I would like to talk to you sometime about your work. I have some ideas on a collaboration we could do in the future. How much longer do you plan on staying in London?" Coco asked without realizing how much this question was so much more complicated than she may realize.

"I was planning to leave in a couple of days, but I think I want to extend my time here a bit. I am just not ready to leave yet." Elle didn't let her gaze leave Liam.

"I'll have my people reach out to you. Meanwhile, I will give you and Bobby Dazzler some time together," Coco teased, and Liam's face turned a bit red.

"Bobby Dazzler, huh? Is that the horrid nickname that caused your face to turn ten shades of red?" Elle teased Liam too.

"Let's tackle that story another time. Besides, I want to walk around the room arm and arm with the most talented, kind, and lovely person I know. I want to see you enjoy this moment, because you have earned it." Liam smiled and kissed the back of Elle's hand as they continued around the room, greeting people, receiving congratulations, and taking photos.

Chapter 36

The night was an absolute success. Axel was so pleased with the show that he thanked Elle and Margaux on several occasions. Axel said that his preliminary sales were the highest of any show since opening his fashion house. With the emotional moment between Elle and her dad, the crowd seemed to linger and chat more than other shows, also spending more money with strategically placed vendors throughout the venue. An hour after the conclusion of the show, the remaining crowd had become a makeshift after-party. When food ran low, Axel ordered takeaway pizza and had it delivered. The DJ offered to keep playing music as long as people remained. People were strewn about the room while some lounged on sofas and others chatted in small groups. Young, old, hipster, artists, and any kind of person could be found talking to someone in the wee hours of morning at this point.

Elle was sitting on a large sofa next to Liam with her feet resting on his lap. Elle was rubbing the back of Liam's neck with her hand while Liam was massaging her tired feet.

Across from Elle and Liam sat Margaux and Callum. They were nearly a carbon copy of Elle and Liam's cozy position. Elle looked discreetly at Margaux with her eyes, almost questioning if there was a connection between them. Elle was wondering if there may be a little interest between the two of them after all the time they had spent together and their cozy sitting on the sofa. Plus, Callum did invite Margaux to go to Italy for a few days for a post-show celebration. Elle wondered if there may be more than what she thought between the two of them.

Sitting across from Elle, Margaux mouthed a fervent "no" to Elle without Liam or Callum noticing the discreet communication between the women.

Elle's smile widened but she couldn't help wondering for a moment if there was something more between them too.

"Where did your dad go?" Margaux asked Elle. "Is he still around?"

"He went back to his hotel. We are going to spend some time together tomorrow one on one. We were able to chat briefly, but this wasn't the place to chat. I am looking forward to speaking with him tomorrow," Elle continued rubbing a very-relaxed Liam's neck.

"Not to sound forward, but did your mom come too?" Margaux asked out of genuine curiosity.

"Can I take this one?" Liam asked Elle.

"Sure," Elle smiled.

Liam lifted his relaxed head off the sofa and opened his eyes to answer. "Mom is terrified, like terrified of flying on airplanes, but she came. Mom is actually back at the hotel. She knew that Elle and her dad needed their moment tonight to make amends." Liam closed his eyes again and relaxed his head back on the sofa.

Margaux said, "I had a high school friend who was terrified of trains. He hated trains. Thankfully, there weren't many in our area, but he was terrified when we used to go over a railroad crossing. He hated airplanes too. When I moved to NYC, I actually thought about him. I thought about how he would never get to see the world, because he let his fear control him." Margaux's tone seemed to have a tone of confession and left Elle wondering who this friend was that Margaux thought about often.

"That's pretty deep there, Margaux," Elle said to her friend and coworker. Margaux seldom mentioned her past or what led her to New York City. She only expressed the goal was to have as many experiences as possible when she arrived.

"Speaking of seeing the world, I think we have a plane to catch in just a few short hours to Italy. I am not, however, afraid to take a train or a plane to Italy. Who is ready for some fresh pasta and limoncello?" Callum nearly jumped up from the couch and held out a hand to Margaux.

Elle wasn't sure what to make of Callum and Margaux. She wondered if he was flirting with her or just genuinely giddy about the evening. The two of them went along so well.

"Lucy and I are heading to Paris for a few days," Elle said with groggy enthusiasm. "I can't believe I just said that I am going to Paris for a few days. What actual person says anything like that in real life and not in a movie?" Elle asked no one in particular. Margaux nodded enthusiastically, giving a non-verbal answer to Elle's rhetorical question.

"Come on, Boss Lady, and give me a hug goodbye. It is going to be strange not seeing you for a few days. You are one of my favorite people in the world after all." Margaux pulled Elle up from off the sofa and into a hug. "I am so thankful for you," Margaux whispered to Elle. "You have helped me check so many boxes off my list since moving to New York City. Plus, you are not only a mentor, but a dear friend," Margaux continued in a whisper so only the two could hear the conversation. Margaux gave her friend another tight squeeze before letting go.

"Love you, sweet friend. You are a treasure to me too," Elle said in a big sister tone. "I have the information Callum gave me for your trip, so text when you get settled. You are going for about five days or maybe to a week, right? I am thinking of sticking around for an extra week too," Elle admitted.

"I will text when I arrive, and we can coordinate about going back to the States," Margaux confirmed. "Don't go getting married without me," Margaux joked as she was gathering her things to leave.

Margaux and Callum were out the door, and Elle noticed that the crowd really began to thin out.

Elle and Liam continued lounging on the sofa. Their hands were interlocked, and Elle leaned on Liam's shoulder.

"Liam, thank you for bringing my dad here," Elle whispered.

"I'll admit that I didn't know if he would be willing to hear me out, but I wanted to try. Thankfully, he was really open to it and he seemed to really carry a lot of regret too. Plus, I wanted to talk to him face to face. I was hoping he would come here, but if not, I would go see him in the States. Either way, I need to have a conversation with him," Liam continued without pause.

"Is everything okay?" Elle asked Liam, somewhat sitting up from the sofa.

"I just want to speak to him," Liam continued with his eyes closed, attempting to be nonchalant.

"Please don't feel like you have to defend me with my dad. I want to have a relationship with my dad, but I am not going to defend who I am to get his approval. Dad needs to take me for who I am. I am not the same broken girl I was a few years ago that felt nothing but rejection from her parents. Don't get me wrong, it still does hurt a bit, but I am more confident in who I am, and I know I have strong convictions, even if my parents don't see it. You don't have to defend me to my father," Elle said with a firm but appreciative tone.

"I was not going to defend you," Liam continued.

"What were you going to say to him?" Elle demanded.

"I was going to talk about our future." Liam kept his eyes closed and relaxed.

Liam opened his eyes. "I wanted to invite them to be part of our future. When I fell for you, I knew you were it. I don't need anyone else in my life. I am the luckiest man in the world. I don't need anyone else, but I would like to have your parents in our lives because I know it would mean so much to you. God has been doing a work in me through you, and I told your dad that. I wanted him to know that you are continuing to do God's work, even if he couldn't see it, and it isn't just on me," Liam said as he looked lovingly into Elle's eyes.

"I wanted to let your dad know that I have found the person I want to spend my life with, and I hope they want to be part of our lives," Liam continued.

"I feel the same way about you." Elle pulled Liam into a standing hug, and both of them were holding onto one another.

"One day, I am going to propose to you, Elle Bennett. You are my person. I want it to be the perfect moment when I do," Liam whispered in her ear as they continued to hug in the room, sounded with workers cleaning up and about twenty randomly strewn people about the room.

"Today was a pretty perfect day. I am not sure what would be the perfect moment, but I love you too," Elle smiled.

"If you think it is a perfect time, I won't waste another minute." Liam got down on one knee in the middle of the room while settling down on one knee. "Elle, will you make me the happiest bloke on earth? You continue to inspire me with your kindness and good heart. You work so hard and are so talented. You inspire me to be a better person. I hope I can be an inspiration to you too. I can't believe you would even take a chance on someone like Bobby Dazzler." Liam's smile widened even more as he joked about his unfortunate nickname.

"Yes, Liam, I will marry you." Elle kissed Liam while bending down and holding her hands on either side of his face.

Liam slipped the ring he had been hiding in his jacket onto Elle's delicate finger. Liam stood and picked up Elle into his arms, and the rest of the room erupted into applause.

Chapter 37

Within moments of saying yes, Elle's phone began dinging non-stop with notifications that she was receiving text messages.

Liam's phone began to ring.

Then, Elle's phone began ringing too.

"Did I just watch you get engaged?" Liam could hear a very irritated voice on the other end of the phone.

"Hello Lucy, yes, you did see me get engaged. It was a little spur of the moment decision," Liam continued.

"I get your point, Lucy. Technically, I had the ring in my pocket, so it must have been something I had been thinking about, but I didn't plan on doing it today. You are right; I have been thinking of marrying this amazing woman. I was still trying to find the perfect place and time, but suddenly, it became the perfect place and time. I know … I know. Thank you. I love you too." Liam smiled. "I am a lucky man. I'll talk to you soon." Liam hung up the phone and began listening to Elle's conversation while holding her newly engaged hand and running gentle kisses up her hand.

Elle answered her phone. "Yes, we did get engaged. How on earth did you find out we got engaged?" Elle asked. "Oh, I see him in the back of the room. Thanks for going live, Axel … I am now in trouble with my people for not waiting until they were here for the engagement!" Elle said sarcastically as she raised her voice so that Axel could hear her from across the room. "I am actually shocked. Liam said it was one of the reasons he wanted to meet my dad so that he could talk to him about our future plans as a couple." Elle looked at a smiling Liam who just got off of his phone and was gently kissing her hand as she chatted. "I wish you could have been here too, but I tell you what, you will be at the most important thing, the wedding. After all, you know that I would want you to be my maid of honor, right?" Then Elle held the phone away from her ear. Elle looked at Liam and mouthed, "She does this tea-kettle squeal that is brutal on the ears on the phone."

Elle put her ear back on the receiver once the sound subsided.

"Of course, honey, I love you too. You mean so much to me. Oh ok, have a great time on your trip. I am glad you made it through security, and you are about to board the plane. Big hugs and love you," Elle hung up the phone.

"Are Callum and Margaux on the plane already?" Liam asked in his all-too-protective voice, clarifying that people he cared about were safe.

"They are on the plane, and Margaux is about to shut down her phone so not to worry. First, she had to voice her many complaints about not being here for the big engagement, but she quickly seemed to have forgiven me after I asked her to be the maid of honor. Wait, oh my gosh, I want Lucy to be the maid of honor too. Is that a thing?" Elle asked Liam, almost laughing about the predicament. She didn't care either way. She would make it a thing to have two maids of honor.

"You poor baby, you have so many people who adore you that you struggle with juggling your fans," Liam teased.

The couple plopped themselves back down on the sofa again. This time, Liam's arm was draped around Elle's shoulders, and she kept looking at the beautiful princess cut ring on her finger.

A ding sound came from Elle's phone, *We are literally going to be sisters!!! I can't believe it! Love you!* Elle read Lucy's message aloud and smiled.

"Your sister can't wait to be my sister soon too." Elle smiled even bigger and leaned to kiss Liam again. Liam and Elle were relaxed on the sofa and soaking in the absolutely magical evening.

"Excuse me, I am looking for Margaux." Elle and Liam were interrupted by a person standing in front of them. He was a tall, broad-shouldered American standing in front of them.

"Hello, I'm sorry. Did you say you were looking for Margaux?" Elle was almost bewildered that someone outside of their fashion world bubble knew Margaux here in London.

"I'm sorry, she left already. Can I help you with anything?" Elle looked at the man who had a concerned look on his face. Elle tried to take in his features. He appeared to be about six feet tall, broad-shouldered, and sandy brown hair. He looked concerned but didn't appear aggressive. He seemed insistent.

"Is everything okay?" Elle pressed.

"Do you know when she will be back?" he asked.

"She won't be back for a few days because she took a trip to Italy to celebrate the end of our show." Elle realized she may be sharing too much because she didn't know who this person was standing in front of her with a distinguishable American accent.

"She went to the Amalfi Coast, didn't she?" he asked again without answering who he was.

At this point, Liam's protective instincts began kicking in and he asked, "I'm sorry, who are you?" This time, Liam was standing up, after realizing the man was not answering any of the questions Elle asked him about who he was and why he was looking for Margaux.

The man seemed almost nostalgic suddenly. He didn't answer again who he was or why he was there to see Margaux.

"She was always obsessed with the Amalfi Coast, New York, London, or any place that was not Indiana," he said with a forlorn look.

"Look mate, I don't know who you are or why you have come, but it is clear you aren't telling us who you are. I think you need to leave because we aren't telling you anything about Margaux's whereabouts if we don't know why you need to see her," Liam insisted.

"I am her fiancé," he answered matter-of-factly. "I want to see her. That is all I want," he said calmly.

Both Liam and Elle stood looking at one another, completely dumbfounded by what they just heard. They watched the mysterious man walk out of the room and out of the exit.

Chapter 38

Elle and Liam silently stared at one another for at least two minutes, absolutely shocked by what they had just heard.

"I had no idea Margaux was engaged. She never talks about anyone from her hometown. I have never seen a ring or a text that would suggest that there was someone in her life. I am absolutely shocked."

Elle grabbed her phone to text Margaux and let her know what just happened.

"She won't find out about him being here until she lands in Italy. I don't think he was angry, do you?" Elle asked Liam, trying to get a gauge on how she read him.

"No, he didn't seem angry at all. He seemed heartbroken honestly. He acted like he just wants to see her, but I am wondering why Margaux would leave her hometown if her fiancé was there." Liam was trying to deduce the motivations of Margaux.

"Well, he clearly is not the friend who was afraid of trains and planes because he had to ride all of those to be standing here, most likely," Elle attempted a joke.

"I messaged her, so she should get the message when she arrives in Italy. I wonder how he found out she was here specifically?" Elle's imagination was getting the best of her.

"Margaux is always on social media, so I am guessing they are still friends or that they have mutual friends. I don't think Margaux is the type of person to avoid being on social media even if she left a fiancé behind. Plus, I could see her actually remaining friends with an old boyfriend. She is just a social person, so I think it would be easy to find her," Liam observed.

"Do you think he would try to find her in Italy?" Elle asked.

"He made it all the way here to London to see her, so I wouldn't be surprised if he tried to find her there too. I mean, what is a little more traveling when you want to see the person you love?" Liam responded and suddenly the conversation returned to Elle and Liam.

"I texted her so I don't think there is any more we can do to-night," Elle said, shrugging her shoulders.

"I think I need to escort the most coveted stylist in London back to her hotel for a good night's rest. Then, I want to pick her up in the morning so that she can spend time with her mom and dad. Hopefully, I can spend more time with you guys too before you head to Paris with my sister." Liam pulled Elle closer to him.

Both of them stood facing one another with their arms casually draped around one another.

"What kind of timeline did you have for this engagement when you asked me?" Elle asked Liam.

"What kind of timeline? I have no idea. I was just hoping you wouldn't tell me no when I asked," Liam joked.

"One thing that I don't think you know about me is that I love Christmas," Elle confessed. "Did you know that surprising fact about me?"

"Actually, I think I noticed a Christmas tree in your shop the night we met," Liam mentioned as the space was coming back to him. "I thought you were quite late in getting your decorations put away," Liam teased, thinking it was August.

"I always dreamt of getting married at Christmas time." Elle smiled conspiratorially.

"A Christmas wedding is what you want?" Liam again smiled.

"This makes me wonder, would we want a year-long engagement to figure out all of the logistics of our lives together? This is what most sensible people would choose. Then again, we could choose to have a wedding this Christmas if we are completely out of our minds. I mean, who attempts to pull a wedding together so quickly?" Liam looked at Elle. Elle was trying to decide if he was joking or actually suggesting they get married in just four months' time.

Elle's stomach fluttered thinking of how she dreamt of having a Christmas wedding. She would love time to plan an extravagant wedding with Liam. Then again, she was in her late twenties and eager to start her happily ever after, so planning a wedding in just four months would be enticing just so that they can begin their lives together earlier.

"You know the perfect place to have a Christmas wedding," Liam asked.

"The North Pole?" Elle joked.

"Germany," Liam answered, completely serious.

"We could find the charming German town in the midst of the Christmas market season. We could host our dearest friends in a charming chalet for the event," Liam continued.

Elle marveled at how well he knew her and could envision a wedding since she was a very young girl.

Elle couldn't help but respond, "In that case, we better get married in four months because I don't think I can stay away from you much longer than that," Elle answered, even surprising herself.

With that, Liam pulled her to him. They embraced one another, as he placed her hands on either side of Elle's face. Then, softly, his lips met hers. The world around them faded away, leaving just the two of them in that perfect, suspended moment. His kiss was gentle while Elle's heart swelled, and she responded, her lips moving against his with growing emotion. Their kiss deepened, a dance of tenderness and unspoken emotion. She felt the heat of his touch, the way his hand slid around her waist, pulling her closer. Then, they pulled away from one another, looking lovingly into one another's eyes.

"I love you," Liam whispered.

"I love you more," Elle teased.

"Now, let's plan a Christmas wedding." Liam smiled and lifted Elle into his arms and spun her in a small circle.

Epilogue

Margaux walked down the long aisle of the airplane, counting down the numbers softly to herself while looking for her seat. Callum found his seat toward the front of the plane; he also opted for the airplane's cheapest seats like Margaux. Sure, both earned some sizable bonuses from the fashion show, but they were both used to living modestly, and both were pleased with themselves for finding last-minute airline tickets for such a great price.

Margaux continued down the aisle, trying to be mindful of her sizable backpack that narrowly missed hitting each person sitting in the aisle seat. She found her seat 24B and soon realized she was placed in … the middle seat. She hated the middle seat because the window person controlled the opening and the closing of the window shade. Who chooses to sit by the window without taking advantage of the view?

Margaux attempted to squeeze past the long-legged teen who was sitting comfortably in the aisle seat of her row. Appearing slightly annoyed with Margaux moving past him to get to her seat, the teen shifted slightly to allow her past after what appeared to be hesitation.

She sat in the middle seat and shoved her small backpack in front of her in the provided space under the seat in front of her.

Margaux was a little nervous about carrying some of her bonus money, which was given to her in cash, in her backpack. Italy was notorious for pickpockets, and she didn't want to jeopardize this little extra money that she earned. She reminded herself that she needed to be vigilant with her belongings during her trip.

Margaux took a deep breath and put her head back on her seat. She snapped her seatbelt across her waist and finally allowed herself to rest. Remembering her phone was still turned on, she pulled out her device and switched on airplane mode. Then, she closed her eyes, put her head back, and began to really relax. Margaux was so thankful for some down time, and sitting in this seat was the first bit of rest she felt like she had had in days but what felt like weeks.

Just as she was feeling her body begin to unwind, Margaux felt a tapping on her shoulder. She opened her eyes and saw a middle-aged woman stand by the annoyed teen slightly bent over while standing in the aisle so that she was eye-level to Margaux. "Excuse me, would you mind changing seats with me?" the woman requested.

"I'm sorry." Margaux was a bit confused why this woman would request changing seats with her or if she was asking the teen to change seats. No one typically volunteered themselves for the middle seat, let alone, the middle seat in the cheap seats of the airplane.

"Oh, I am sorry." The woman realized how out of nowhere her question may have come, so she continued, "This is my son and I was hoping we could sit together. The airline mixed up our seats, and we were separated in the airplane. Do you mind changing seats with me? They actually put me in business class for some reason, so you will be able to sit in business class if you change seats with me," the woman explained.

Margaux wanted to confirm what she thought she heard because this offer sounded too good to be true.

"You want me to change seats with you so you can sit with your son? My new seat will be in business class?" Margaux thought she must have misunderstood the woman.

"Yes, please. If you are willing to change, I will be sure to let the flight attendants know that you have agreed to switch seats," the woman confirmed. "My son is a bit of a nervous flier..." The annoyed teen's eye widened after his mom offered this personal information with Margaux.

"I would be happy to switch with you," Margaux agreed rather quickly. She gathered her things and made sure she took her backpack but was thinking about yet another box she was going to check off her life to-do list. She was greeted by a friendly flight attendant who led Margaux to her new seat in the business class. Margaux nearly pranced down the aisle to her new seat. She was sure to wave at a very confused Callum, who was wondering why she was moved to business class and following her with his eyes with a puzzled look on his face. Margaux couldn't believe her eyes. She now had a window seat ... in business class! She placed her items down and quickly got situated before the plane would make its final preparations for takeoff. She pulled up the window shade and admired the tarmac filled with workers making final preparations for their takeoff and smiled contently.

Remembering her "Life's Wishlist" in her backpack, Margaux

dug deep into her backpack and flipped open the journal. Margaux had been adding new items to this list since her trip to London to work as an assistant lead stylist for a fashion show. She would have never imagined that she would have moved to New York months ago. She opened the journals and found the growing list in front of her. She smiled as she looked at the list she began when she was twelve years old. Of course, she upgraded her journal, but the idea remained the same. Margaux scanned the list and saw "fly business class" on the list. She drew a satisfying single line through the item on the list so that she can still see it and appreciate the blessing of it when she saw the list again. She closed her journal and put her book away. Then, Margaux returned to watching the activity outside of the window, as if she had never been on an airplane before today. She was soaking in the moment.

An attentive flight attendant brought a menu for food, drinks, and creature-comfort options that business class guests could request once they were at cruising altitude. Margaux had never been in business class and couldn't believe she could order from this menu for little or no additional cost. She quickly learned that the menu was in Italian; however, she had no idea what she was looking at on the beautifully designed page.

"I can't read any of this," Margaux said to herself. "It's all in Italian. Do they have an English menu?" Margaux continued talking to herself because the flight attendant had already moved to the next patron.

"Do you make it a habit of talking to yourself?" A voice asked her with a playful, but friendly tone.

"I talk to myself sometimes, but I don't answer back," Margaux deadpanned without looking in his direction while searching for an *Italian for Beginners* book she picked up in the airport.

"Did I hear you say that you had trouble reading the menu? I can help translate if you would like," the voice continued.

"Sure, I would never turn down help when I clearly need it," Margaux attempted with some self-deprecating humor to make this awkward situation less awkward.

The man sitting next to her leaned over and pointed at the menu. Margaux took in his almost soapy, citrus scent. She saw his smile widen as he looked at Margaux while simultaneously pointing at the menu with hopeful eyes. Then, he realized his manners once Margaux looked in his direction.

"By the way, my name is Giovanni." His Italian accent was subtle, but present. He held out his hand and shook Margaux's hand.

It wasn't until now that Margaux really looked at him. His olive skin, his wavy well-styled hair, and beautiful eyes.

"Margaux," she said, while attempting to remain nonchalant while shaking hands with one of the most attractive men she has ever seen in her life…

About the Author
Michelle Tibbs-Brown

About The Author Michelle Tibbs-Brown Michelle Tibbs-Brown is a first-time author who has been in love with love from the moment she saw the Cinderella movie at a drive-in theater as a child. Michelle plans to continue the stories of characters in this book. When Michelle isn't working or writing, she is planning another budget-minded trip for her family, making a quick trip to Disney, or volunteering in her community. She loves a European breakfast and an adorable cafe. She lives in her "pretty little city" of Saint Petersburg, Florida with her daughter, husband, and toothless Maltipoo, Chanel.